Etash
and the
Cosmic Balance

ISBN 978-81-940285-1-2

Layouts	:	Vidya Hegde
Editing	:	Vidya Hegde
Illustrations	:	Pradnya Shedge

Kindle Edition Published By:

Hasayana Media
A Tanzpuppen Entertainment Pvt Ltd Company

www.tanzpuppen.com

Dedications

Vidya Hegde & Etash Bhat – My inspiration always.

My support system - Appa, Amma, Rashmi & family, Raghuram & family

Ganapathi Bhat – For supporting my endeavours from ideation state through implementation. By the by, he successfully runs a marketing and customer service firm Neojit.

Lunch Group @ office – If not for them, I would not have been patient through the entire cycle of publication.

Friends since childhood – Nitin, Subbu, Nibejoy.

About the author

I was born in Uppinangadi, a small town about 30 KM from the well-known Mangalore city. People from anywhere in the coastal belt would call themselves Mangaloreans. Having spent my entire childhood in a multi-cultural township called Kudremukh, the most important binding factor for me to call myself a Mangalorean is the rich cuisine. I would prefer a wholesome meal made of boiled rice, *patrode*, *melara*, white *tonde kaayi*, the larger *bende kaayi* and *kaayi holige* to any star cuisine.

The writing bug in me started late. Very late compared to when the reading bug caught up. During childhood, we kids used to get together at my grandfather's place, Vadyadagaya, for summer holidays. I was one of the younger ones in the group. In the midday, we used to gather in the attic and read my uncle's huge collection of books. Of course, I did not know how to read. I used to count the words just to feel part of the group. Later I managed to learn to read and then managed to read all the books in the local library. This is when the writing bug caught up. I started writing small stories in Hindi. My Hindi teacher was very encouraging. He said, "You write well, though you do not have a good hold on the language!" To be fair I never understood the nuances of grammar in any language. The saga of my writing continued through writing diaries and then stopped when I realised the breach of privacy. My diary had been read!

Around a decade, back I got back into writing blogs. It started as a way for me to vent my frustrations: lack of development in my area, lack of recognition at work and sometimes-plain old hormonal imbalance.

Around mid of 2018, a few months since launch of my Wife's ambitious company, Tanzpuppen, I created a small animation movie. Looking at the badly done animation movie with an interesting script, my brother in law encouraged me to rather try my hand at making this a novel.

During this time I was watching *Yog* on TV, my weekend morning routine. (I have been brought up to believe in hard work. I was hoping to gain some benefit of hard work watching people work hard). I sit on the sofa comfortably as I watch my father Mr. NT Bhat do the entire Yog routine. My mind was sufficiently empty. I was sipping warm water and thinking of nothing, as usual. The universe noticed this and found something to fill my mind with. It filled my mind with a brain wave. I'm living the aftermath of this brain wave for last almost a year. This can only end with the publishing of this book.

The plot for the novel is entirely a work of fiction. Several people may see a reflection of their lives in some of the characters. Do trust me, it is simply a coincidence. I believe that stories have a life and you identifying with a character is just a way for the story to communicate with you. Ofcourse, sometimes the story can suck the reader in and then the difference between the story and the world fades away. Atleast, that's my theory, which ofcourse is totally a figment of my imagination.

I wanted to publish the novel by January 2019, 4 months since I had started writing. Not knowing the nuances of publishing, I had assumed it to be as easy as writing bad emails, not reviewing before sending them and then being troubled for the next few months. At about this time, I started working on an ambitious project at the office. I could not devote much time to my sweetheart - this novel. My other sweet heart, my wife Vidya, stepped in and worked hard at making the trash that I had churned out into the gold that is currently in your hands. This story definitely has a life. It knew exactly how it wanted itself published. It planned everything to the tee. I'm thankful to this story for finding me.

Mahesh can be reached at : info@hasayana.net

Preface

We are a blessed generation. We have come from a time when there were no telephones and no televisions in our houses. We have even lived in homes with no electricity at our grandparents in the village. We have witnessed the change from nothing to high configuration mobiles and 60-inch televisions. All this in just about 40 years! Such is the pace of scientific advancement.

We humans have conquered space, reached the far end of the galaxy and gone beyond. We have answers to almost everything. We apparently have a vague idea about the beginning of it. It almost certainly started with a big bang, and now the entire universe is expanding into an ever-increasing available space. We have proof that the universe is expanding. We can surmise that at one point the expansion may stop. We can surmise that there may be a great collapse. We can also surmise there could be an expansion after that. Today, we have the means to make the right surmises!

We now know that the laws of physics work very well for the huge outer space. The inner world of things, however, the tiny part, quantum to be precise -this is where our laws have bungled. The scientists were troubled! - Until the advent of Quantum Theory, that tells us that there is something called a 'Positron', which takes the position of observation. Thank *Paramaatma* for that, we now have a profound understanding of the Quantum world.

Questions like what existed before the big bang are not relevant in the large scheme of things.

Some sages, very long ago, sat below trees in thick forests and seemed to do nothing. However, they spoke about the concept of the multiverse! They said there were several universes. They talked about the cyclic nature of 'time.' In fact, they went on to say that there cannot be an absolute start of time. Of course, that must have been just some kind of lucky guesswork. Afterall how would they have known such concepts by just sitting below a tree!

The spiritualists have believed in the omnipresence of *Paramaatma*. In *Bhagavad Gita*, Arjuna saw the diversity of *Paramaatma* manifested in the entire creation. Different religious texts state this in different ways - *Paramaatma* can be found where a true believer seeks. The similarities between the concepts of Positrons, and a power that resides wherever a human sees the power, is probably just coincidental as well.

The sages again imagined the living organisms to be an embodiment of this multiple universes. "*Aham Brahmasmi*" _ I have no duality. There is no instrument by which I know my existence or my otherness, except in a *jeeva* or in a state of incarnation. I am in all, and all are in me.

The outer- the huge- unknown space and the inner- vast - unknown space were thought to reflect each other _ *Aatma* is *Brahman*. This has been further illustrated as Indra's net, which is a metaphor used to describe the interconnectivity between the celestial beings. At least in this aspect then there is no coincidence of similarities between a *yogi* and a scientist. We do not have a central system with several atoms revolving around. We do not have heat-generating body part - Thank *Paramaatma* for that. We can have a good night's sleep knowing very well that we are in safe hands of science. A few coincidences of theories can well be ignored. Some concepts like Quantum entanglement should not give us a nightmare.

To a sufficiently unscientific and general mind like mine, several theories seemed very similar: '*Kundalini*' Awakening, 'Positrons,' 'Quantum Space,' '*Tripura Rahasya*,' 'Quantum Entanglement,' '*Aham Brahmasmi*,' and '*Advaita*.'

Character-o-graphy

The main universe: The universe where concepts related to thought travel unravels.

The orphan universe: A term coined for the novel. It is the place where a parallel storyline is developing.

Troika: Buffalo, Professor and Wind-man; they have been together since time immemorial. They have fought many wars against evil.

Etash: A mild-mannered gentleman with extraordinary powers.

Inu: A not so mild-mannered lady with extraordinary powers.

Patali: A powerful group that has challenged Troika for ages. They want to upset the balance of the multiverse.

Chair-man: A very shrewd strategist, at least he imagines himself to be shrewd. He is working for the Kingdom.

Web-man: A shrewd strategist, again, only the reader can judge his shrewdness. He is the lead for Yuvan and the star-boy.

Yuvan: A mild-mannered gentleman. A weapon in the hands of everyone and anyone who can lay their hands on him.

Isha: A very strong lady with very strong opinions. She is Yuvan's companion throughout his journey.

Kingdom: An unknown place somewhere in the orphan universe. Do they have a king?

Council of ministers: Some strategists who run the kingdom. There is hardly anything left to the imagination of the reader here. They are true strategists.

Star-boy: Web-man's protege. He has a lot of
imagination. He imagines a very secure kingdom and
believes in it.

Etash's self-realization travel

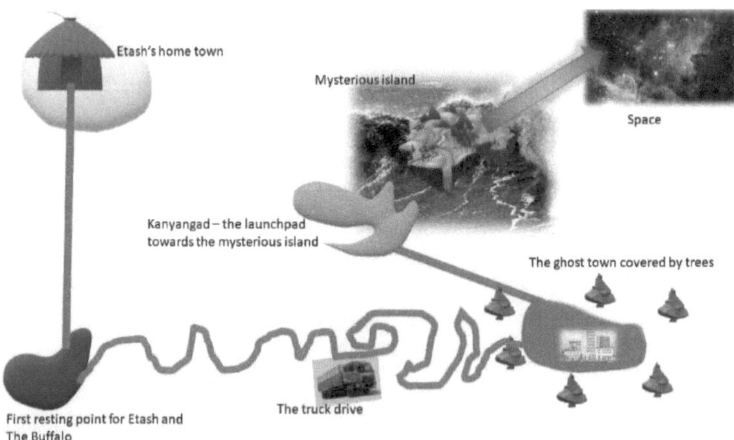

Surapura to Kingdom — Road Map

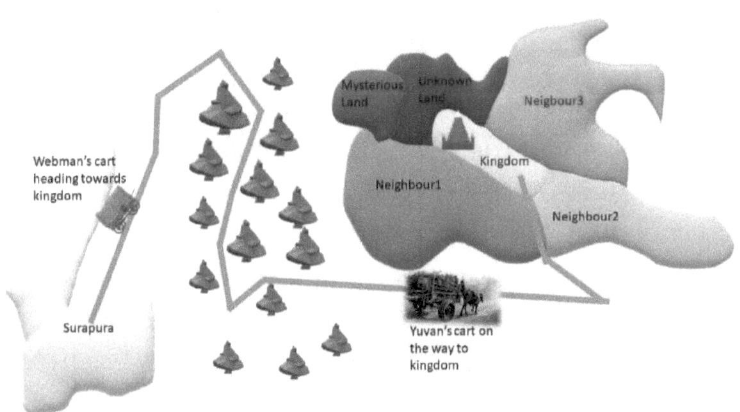

At different places in the multiverse...

The rains were like never before in the rural Badlands of Pagunda. He stood on his balcony facing north. Water droplets hit his military cap like pins. He thought, "Power...I want power. I want to rule the universe." There was thunder. A lightening followed that seemed to hit his cap. He turned back. He had a grin...a grin of a savage.

Somewhere, some other time, the rains were like never before in the peaceful city of Mochileon. He was standing on a hillock in the town of Brinjingarten. "Power! I want power!" Lightning followed a big thunder; hit his trademark military cap sliding down onto his mustache.

Another time, another day, the rains always seemed like never before. He stood at a beach. "Power!" Same thunder and lightning...this time it hit ten heads at a time. The grin was ten times more horrible.

In a very modern time, somewhere in the crowded city of *Bengaluru*. He stood next to his cubicle. The AC in his office was on full blast. He lifted his hands towards the ceiling and cried, "Power!" There was a crackling and then a sizzling, his monitor sparked-hitting his bald head. Now the man dialled a number and started speaking, "I assume everyone in your team comes in this Sunday. I want no exception." The man dialled another number with even more confidence. "Sir, we are on it, I will look into all the defects. You ask for next week; I will deliver tomorrow." Another number, "I don't see any leads in the team. However, I will mentor someone junior and try to bring him up. Maybe in a few years..." The man's grin was maniacal.

Chapter 1

Somewhere, at some point in a multiverse, as good as any universe next door - a kingdom, as good as any next-door kingdom!
From a random point of observation, one can see a person. One can make out the aura he shed — an aura of an all-important person. Sitting on 'the chair' brought this kind of aura to anybody. He was given 'the chair.' The tag had come along with it.
"I'm the greatest. I have made the king. I have made this kingdom…"
The Chair-man turned towards the window. He had a cabin facing a beautiful lake.
"I will make this kingdom an empire. I will ask the king to attack the country to the left first, and then right and then left…and then right, and then left and then right and then…

"I am sleeping aren't I?"

"Why am I asking myself a question while asleep? I'm not in my usual disturbed sleep state, or I would toss and turn, won't I?"

Etash observed the movement of his eye and the fetal position that he always slept in. He did seem sound asleep.

"Wait a minute! How do I see myself while asleep?"

What was that sharp light at the corner of the room beckoning him? The urge to follow the light was irresistible. He pursued his instinct and went into the tunnel. There was a sudden tug. It pulled him inside with great force. He felt like a littered paper being sucked into a vacuum cleaner. Before he could realize his panic…it all calmed down. He was now in a dark tunnel with blue light all over. It was freezing. He realized he should have shivered to his bones. However, it was just that - a realization. The body actually felt nothing. As he went ahead, he noticed some LED screens on the wall. An interesting tunnel this was. Something like an underwater aquarium. As he moved forward, he saw that they were proper LED TV. Each TV was playing some movie. They were not right though. Instead of Madhuri dancing for *'Dhak Dhak,'* it was Shilpa Shetty. Somebody needed to polish his or her knowledge of Bollywood.

"Hold on!" he said to himself. He sure wasn't here to solve some Bollywood riddle!

"Why are you here then?" Came a voice from one of the TV panels.

"Hmm, somebody is guiding me here." he thought. "Who are you?"

He expected some saintly type person to appear with an explosion and through a cloud. Questions like "Who are you?" demanded such dramatic entries. Usually, thunder would follow! In addition, with lightning, there should have been a special appearance!

However, nature did not work quite like in the normal world here!! Etash though was too confused to understand anything. He looked around and was startled!! The video on the screen was of him!

"I'm your subconscious thought," it said!!

With that, the tunnel suddenly ended. The door opened, and he found himself in a ghostly town. It looked like a remote town, Bijauli, he had visited several times as a child. There was no one around though. There were a few vehicles parked on the road here and there.

He slowly walked on and arrived near a mango grove. As he entered the groove, he saw a buffalo, swinging upside down, from a branch right in front of him. The Buffalo, as huge as they usually are, was swinging from the tree by its tail! It seemed to be smiling, which is probably the only expression a buffalo can have or can you call it a smirk?!!

"Hello!" it said.

"Hello!?" Etash wished back.

"So?"

"Why are you swinging upside down?"

"Really? That's the question you want to ask me right now. , Not – "Who are you?" or "What am I doing here?", or "what are you doing here?""

"OK, then, well, why are you here?"

"Because this is as good a place to be as anywhere else."

This seemed deliberate; The Buffalo was trying to get on his nerves.

"Why am I here?"

"How am I to know?!!!"

"Pointless conversation!" he thought to himself as he felt the anger. He wasn't sure why he was angry though. While he was still trying to figure out what he was feeling, he felt a tug. He was being pulled back into the tunnel. The tunnel sucked him in and then spit him out into his bedroom. He was thrown back into his body with a thud. It was as if somebody has physically ejected him from his dream.

He sat on his bed shocked. "What just happened?"

Chapter 2

Two people are engaged in a discussion. It seems to be very intense. They seem to be people who are worried about the welfare of humanity. For a distant observer, the discussion seems to be about a grave danger to humanity.

"No Bro, that won't do. It would easily be found." The man seems to be obsessed with the web. He has a sticky web on his hands that he is twiddling as he spoke. He looks like a subordinate to the other man.

"Then how about we start off on a Thursday and come back Sunday. Everybody is happy." The other man who had so far seemed like the boss looked a bit meek when he spoke.

"Do you think Friday will be good?" The man with the web on his hand somehow appears to be a bossy subordinate.

"Friday will be awesome bro. We shall reach the party venue by Friday morning. We can arrange everything by evening."

"I just love working for you, sir. I just hope my wife doesn't find out." The man with the web, one can call him a Web-man for want of a simple term, has clearly addressed the other man as sir.

"Ah! No chance. I will get my wife to call your wife. It will look all very official. You just keep working

with me. You will see where you reach in a few years."
For anybody at an earshot, it was clear that they were planning to cheat their spouses. Nobody was at earshot though. They knew where and when to plan.

"Awesome!"

"Also, in the long term, you need to have a uniform. Something people can identify you with. I prefer my people to shed an aura." The boss asserted he is the boss by addressing the Web-man as "my people."

"Like?"

"Well, the Superman wears a red cape. The Batman has a black cape."

"Hmm,.I will think about it." The Web-man said deep in thought. He had liked the idea of having a uniform.

Quantum Mechanics had always been a topic of Etash's interest. At least since the time, his grandfather told him the story of *Sushena* and *Mahasena*. He had a Sanskrit edition of the story, which he carefully preserved behind the prayer dome at home. As he fondly recalled his grandfather, he realized it was almost time for his favorite class – philosophy and physics. Physics and Philosophy is a demanding and rewarding course, combining the most rigorous and fundamental subjects in the arts and the sciences. It seeks an understanding of the nature of reality and of our knowledge of it. There are strong links between physics and philosophy, and the stimulus for each discipline lies in part in the other.

The Professor was still at the broader subjects, like the anti-matter. Today, in particular, he was speaking about an exciting notion – a story has a life.

"A story has a life…" The Professor did that. Giving a gap to dramatize his statements. It was his thing.

"…and we are just a part of it. The universe is not about humans. Humans are part of the universe. Universe happened for a purpose. We are part of that purpose. As humans, this would hit our ego. It is too much to accept. We want to feel ourselves to be important in the scheme of things. What if it is the story that is important? A big story of *Kaliyug* is unravelling at this point in time. The story of *Kaliyug* requires many bad things to happen. The bad people are instruments in this. "

Again the gap, a dramatic one.

"Each one, each character involved with this story, one would think had an independent life. However, if you look at it from here, today, they are all part of a big epic."

With a deep breath, The Professor continued, "I'm sure this topic would bring a lot of unease. If we are just some pawns in the bigger picture, why do we have to bother about anything, do we? Bad people are bad because somebody made them bad or they had to be bad to serve a greater purpose. We don't have to punish them, do we?"

Etash had thought a lot about fate and human energy. He thought about this differently. "Probably one can choose one's part in the big story. Since each of us is a pawn, we can slowly build a small chapter for ourselves that is sufficiently comfortable and makes us happy. When there is a big flood, it would definitely not be possible to swim against it. Maybe if we carve a small canal out of this, we may be able to swim into calmer water as we watch the big flood go by. "

"That is an interesting thought Etash! Have you chosen your project for the semester! Do take this topic further and research on it a bit. An additional point to ponder would be - Can we alter a story's life by providing addendums. Instead of a large frame like *Kaliyug*, consider a small phenomenon like the number of students who would quit my class from tomorrow and can it be changed?" said The Professor looking at the rest of the students who seemed to be sleepy during the boring discussion. The Professor went on about the life of a story. It almost seemed like he was referring to fate. "I understand that you would be mapping this concept to fate. We need to see if unlike fate, one can alter the destination of a story. Think about the topic. Let us debate over this in the next class." The Professor started collecting his material to leave. His class for the day was over.

As he left the class, The Professor, asked Etash to meet him at the library at the end of the day. It was no surprise - professors wanting to speak to him. He was, after all, the star of the class. He probably wanted to discuss some ideas.

Chapter 3

Yuvan was resting. His weapon of choice was too. He was dressed like a superhero, – a turban, a loin cloth and of course his weapon. He seemed pre-occupied. One would wonder if he was plotting his next move against some extra-terrestrial invaders. Some people are like an open book you see, you can read them just by their look.

A man in red walked up to him. He was struggling with his outfit -- tight and covered with web all over. He sat beside Yuvan, neither of them looking at each other, aware of each other's presence though.

"You are a warrior for God's sake!" the Web-man was annoyed.

"I think I am doing OK," said Yuvan serenely.

"You are part of the Warrior practice. You can't be like this. At least wear something decent."

Yuvan stood up, removed the turban, kept it on a branch, and brushed his hair.

"Ok! I'm ready. You are the leader. Lead me. I will do as you say."

The Web-man smiled. They marched, like just out of a comic book - two superheroes marching. An intent listener could hear the drums beating to their march. The universe, in that way, is an entertaining place for keen listeners.

As the classes for the day ended, he picked up his bag and walked towards the library. He felt like someone was following him. He stopped and looked behind. She was right there! He lost his focus and dropped his bag, the books spilled all over. Inu was looking at the books intently.

"Just a few books on time travel, umm, just a few." He was almost defending himself. She smiled. The smile radiated across his heart and transmitted his soul into an alternate dimension…well almost.

She slowly opened her bag; she had almost the same collection! "I may know something" she whispered and then walked off. He kept staring at her until The Professor tapped him on the shoulder. "Hmm! An interesting girl that is. Inu is brilliant. You seem to have chosen a good one."

"What? Me? No, I mean…"

"Let us go to the cafeteria, shall we? I have something important to discuss." The Professor led him into the corridor leading to building 2. The college was housed in a building, which was bought when it was set up. With the growing fame and budget in the past few years, the management felt the need for additional space. The neighboring theatre was converted into a makeshift convention hall, and its waiting area became a cafeteria. The Professor paid for their coffee as he found a seat.

"So? How was it?"

"It was great sir!! You teach well."

"Ok…I know I teach shit! That was not my question. How was your first travel?"

"What?!!!"

"You need some background. This was just your first travel." The Professor took out a small box and gave it to him. "Keep this in your pocket at all times…it will help you keep your sanity in your travels" As they sipped coffee, The Professor let Etash settle with his thoughts.

"Are you saying that it was not a dream? I actually traveled somewhere! How did you know about it?"

"OK! You are not unique! Traveling through thought has been a skill, expertise of several sages in ancient India. In the current day, you would be the 54888th addition to the ever-growing group of thought travellers." He paused and continued in a warning tone. "People sometimes do not know how to come back and get lost forever in this thought world. Earlier the sages would guide their disciples through the thought and bring them back. People without guidance and weaker will power may end up in a coma in the current world. Seeing the risks, we seniors in the group devised a plan. The key thought points have a sensor placed that sends out a signal to detect the presence of the traveller. At the edge of the thought..." The Professor noticed Etash looking very confused. "It is probably too much detail right now. Just have confidence that we are watching you and will help you. I have to also tell you that.." He was interrupted by a call on his mobile. He walked off to a corner and spoke for a while in a hushed tone. When he returned, he looked all excited to Etash.

"I have to leave now. We will be in touch. Be extremely careful during your next few travels. Let *Ishwar* guide you!" The Professor seemed like an overexcited child rushing into a play area as he ran out of the cafeteria.

Chapter 4

Yuvan sat loyally. The Web-man stood in a corner. It was a well-adorned cabin. The cabin had a nameplate, with some web below it.

"You have been doing nothing much with your skills!"

The Web-man spoke to Yuvan, looking straight at his eyes. Yuvan was looking down, calculating the number of fingers in his hand. "Yuvan! Please look me in the eye when I speak to you."

Yuvan looked up. "What do you want?"

The Web-man shook his head and came closer "Yuvan, I have told you several times! You belong to warrior practice. We lead from the front. We design proper weapons. We plan wars. We help kings. I have a great opportunity for you."

Yuvan was curious. "What have you got?"

"There are a lot of new weapons of war. We can do so much. We can check the sharpness of the arrow; we can swing the new sword, we can design a new bow."

Yuvan seemed interested.

"Ok, I will assign you a new office. Follow me"

Yuvan walked behind The Web-man. They reached a door. The web man opened it and with a grand hand- gesture.

"I'm sure you will thank me.," he said.

It looked like a workshop; there were hardly any pieces of equipment though. Only a sign that said 'WORKSHOP' and the greasy walls were an indication. There were several old weapons in a corner.

Yuvan decided to keep up his newfound inspiration

Etash was hungry. He kept the book safe on the shelf and took his wallet, which was also safe under the table. He was someone who believed in the safety of items put in a recycle bin, he hardly cared for data security. His entire study thesis was stored there!

As he stepped out, the chill of December-rural-Bengaluru caught him. He went back and brought out his jacket. It was an unusually calm night. Visibility was very low. The street light was barely lighting up the fog around it. He had chosen to live in a place away from the bustle of the city but at a convenient distance from small restaurants and takeaways. For the life of him, he could not cook. Somehow, culinary art had eluded him.

Just a short walk through a weedy pathway from his home, and he would get into a small busy area of his neighborhood. It was pitch dark, it was a little scary. He got a feeling that someone was following him. He rushed through the path. The bright lights from his favorite little diner at the end of his tread was a welcome sight. He loved his suppertime. The end of the day, sitting with a cup of hot cocoa, having a bite of sandwich, and mulling over the day gone by. Tomorrow was going to be a new day, new experiences, and new challenges. He looked around the diner. This was not the rush-hour. He glanced around as he waited to be served. Damn! She just walked in, the epitome of beauty. The grace with which she moved made his heart skip a beat. His lips parted slightly gasping while he stared. Their eyes met, he was embarrassed and looked away.

In this brief moment, he noticed that she had walked in along with that annoying boy from the class.

"Oh, *Paramaatma*! She is coming over! She is coming over! What do I do? What do I do? Be cool! Be Cool!"

He was going through this internal panic attack when Inu came over and said, "Hey Etu!! How are you?"

He took a deep breath! It would have been a tragedy if she had chosen a shorter form of his name.

She did not wait for his answer. "Well, We just got back from a movie. It wasn't great. Total waste of ti........her voice blurred, and all he could see now is how close she was to him, and her lips moving. **Paramaatma**!, she smelled so good!

"Your order, Etash, your order!" , the server trying to get his attention brought him back.

The butterflies in his stomach did not let him relish his sandwich.

He picked up a newspaper hoping to distract himself.

"I always tell my mom about this diner. She is always worried about where and what I eat!" , Inu kept talking as she seated herself at Etash's table. Must have been a few minutes, no wait, "It has been an hour," he thought as he realized. He was licking the ketchup off an otherwise empty plate. This happened to him around her.

 "It was a pleasure talking to you! Please keep your box safe when you travel next. Bye!"

"What did she just say? How? How does she know about the b...?" he was befuddled!

He reached home pretty much not realizing his hop. He opened the door, put away his keys, and went for a change. He just wanted to put on his jammies and drift off to sleep watching his favorite show.

Chapter 5

Somewhere, at the same time, The Chair-man was critically looking at the writing on a wall.

"Hmm! I have to show this wall to the council of ministers and build a story around it. "

He tried to tilt his head. The view didn't seem satisfactory.

"We need a new wall," said The Chair-man, to his companion. The Chair-man had a companion today.

The companion agreed. "The plan for the war hasn't come out impressive. It is probably a problem with the material of the wall. Ask for a new wall, and I will approve the budget. I have been taught that a leader, who cannot read the writing on a wall, will soon be destroyed. Next time, please make the writing a little larger and clearer, so that I can read it."

One could make out the hierarchy here. The Chair-man clearly reported into his companion.

"I plan to go on a trip to Surapura, to visit our offshore office. I will discuss the design for the wall with our warrior practice there. The lead, Mr. Web-man is my friend." The Chair-man needed approval. Another sign that the companion was his manager. The Chair-man was a little distracted though. If one could glance into his mind, one would notice lots of masala dosas there. Of course, Surapura masala dosas being famous for their flavor may not have had anything to do with The Chair-man's request to go there.

The companion thought for a while. "Hmm, do you think The Web-man can help you with the right fonts? The Council of Ministers wants a proper plan for the wars. They don't seem to have a lot of budget. I would need this writing on the wall very lucid."

The Chair-man was jerked out of his train of thoughts. "I hear you, sir. I will discuss several fonts. I also hear that warrior practice has come up with some new ways of presenting thoughts and designs. Will discuss this in detail with The Web-man. Also, I can probably get you some Masala Chicken from there."

The companion clearly seemed enticed with this, although, it was not clear whether a new way of presenting the designs and thoughts was what attracted him. "You better hurry and pack-up then."

Woosh…Woosh….Woosh…Woosh is all he could hear. He felt warm and cozy. He could hear muffled noises of TV. He thought he must be asleep. Wait a minute, why was he floating? He opened his eyes. Everything seemed dark and blurry. He felt an instinct, and he rolled over. He felt tied at the navel, and the cord kept getting in his way. He was a fetus in a womb. "Why?" he thought. "Why on earth was I thinking about being a fetus? Am I in some sub-conscious level? Am I dreaming? or did I astral project into someone's body? He realized it was futile thinking about it. At least this time he knew what was going on. He remembered the box. It wasn't in his hand. He looked around. No sight of the box. He turned around. There it was, floating just like him. He tried to grab it with his little fingers. The minute he got hold of it, zooooooop…! He was back on his bed, in front of his tv which was running his favorite show.

He took a while to get back to normal. He started to feel weak. This time felt intense. All he wanted to do is retire for the day and get some sleep for the rest of the night. But he was sure he needed help. Without a thought, he sent a message to The Professor. Not more than a minute later, he was snoring.

Not very far, several pairs of eyes were looking at him from some unknown dimension. In fact, one couldn't even be sure if the eyes were in pairs.

Chapter 6

Yuvan's motivation was swinging on and off like a pendulum. He picked up the arrow and calculated its sharpness, on the greasy wall. Then he picked up the bow and calculated its range. The greasy wall was all messed up with the calculations.

The Web-man walked in.

"Hey, you are back to your old self! Come on man, I have given you an opportunity of a lifetime, and you are messing it up. Why do you draw all that nonsense stuff on the wall?"

Yuvan noticed a short man with a paunch, next to The Web-man.

"This is The Chair-man. He is here to have a conversation and some tea with me. You better start doing something worthwhile soon."

The Web-man headed out with The Chair-man.

"The writing on the wall, it seemed quite impressive isn't it?" The Chair-man asked The Web-man.

"Meh.!", The Web-man shrugged it off.

"Daybreak feels so good!" thought Etash as he dressed for college. He was looking forward to meeting The Professor. He had not answered Etash's text. He had read it though. Etash had no classes today, only the weekly 'face to face' with The Professors.

The light of the day makes things appear in an entirely different way.

It was roughly a fifteen minutes bus ride to college. Etash loved these fifteen minutes. He could detach himself from his surrounding and feel the solitude even when in a crowd, a unique power he had gained unknowingly.

"Next Stop is Ganganaya College," the bus announcement startled him. He stood up bent to avoid hitting his head against the roof of the bus. He Straightened his bag and tried to wiggle his way out of the cramped seating of the bus. He maneuvered through the crowd to the exit. He was about to get off the bus when he saw Inu entering the bus from the other door. She was waving at him. Looked like she was asking him to get back in the bus. Her wish was his command.

They met somewhere in the center of the bus.

"We are going to a movie. Thought it would be great if you join."

'We' she said? , he thought to himself.

He looked around and saw at least 15 familiar faces from his class. "Oh Dang!" He thought. It was too late to back off now. They had already reached their destination.

Etash wasn't too much into movies. He spent most of his childhood playing cricket and reading books. He did not care much about the larger than life persona, the larger than life problems and primarily the whole larger than life portrayal in the movies.

This one was different though. Sometimes, it's the thought that matters. And someone making something like this was pretty thoughtful.

The ambiance and the theatre and the loud noise ironically felt like white noise to him. His eyelids dropped and slowly the present faded. It seemed effortless this time. The Same tunnel. He reached the end this time though, into what looked like a corridor. A hotel-like corridor, for instance. He started walking. Should he knock on one of the doors? If, yes, which one? Or should he just push open one of them? Again, which one? He inadvertently pushed open one of them. He did not knock.

"Holy moly!, why would you think of this place? There is nothing here. You could have thought of a better point of entry. People think of awesome spots for their entry!! And look at you, always ending up here!!. I hope you brought your box." Said a voice behind him. He knew that voice. He wished it was just his imagination. He turned around hoping against hope that it wasn't him.

He just shook his head. There he was sitting crossed legged, on a corner table.

What a weird sight!

Etash thought maybe if he probed The Buffalo more, he would get some answers

"WHO ARE YOU? Are you my inner self?"

"Ho! Ho! Ho!" said The Buffalo. First, the way he was sitting and now this. What breed of Buffalo was this?

He tried to dial down his emotions. He now understood that after a point, any change would just kick him back to the starting point, and he would have to come back all over again.

"Come on, Don't be this way. Answer me." , he said sardonically.

"You have two choices. Watch 'Juhi' and think from an old man's perspective. I feel like I want lemonade. Lemon is perfect for acidity if taken with salt. Ho Ho Ho"

"Ok! I have had enough! Thank you, you have been of great help."

A buffalo will be a buffalo! What was I expecting?" He felt strong emotions. The next moment, he found himself back on this seat.

He looked around to see if anyone noticed his sudden movement. Inu was looking at him. She winked and smiled. He saw that. However, he did not notice the person at the other corner of the theatre, watching his every move. It was difficult to make out whether it was a person though. It was covered from head to toe in a blanket.

The movie was over. Inu came close as he walked out of the movie hall, and whispered, "The door to my thoughts opens with two knocks.", and she quietly walked off.

This was important information. "Should I write it down?" Etash thought.

He went through the motions for the rest of the day. He could not stop thinking about entering her 'thought' world. He lost all his nerve when she was with him. He hoped at least in the thought world, he would have the courage to tell her how he felt about her. He could not wait to be back home and try the 'two knocks' thing this time.

Chapter 7

The Chair-man was back in his cabin, in the kingdom. His trip had been immensely successful. He had visited several restaurants serving special masala dosas. Incidentally, he had even discussed some great fonts with the Web-man.
"That was a great trip! Web-man is an awesome company. It is always fun with him." He said as he took out his painting box.
His companion seemed happy too as he slurped the chicken masala.
"Some of these colors that The Web-man gifted me are just awesome. He is brilliant. He knows the art of the war. One cannot plot a war without proper tools." he thought, as he held a brush and dipped into one of the colors.
He took utmost care to plot a demarcation in the center of the wall. Then he painted a cross which went across. Now with some red, he sketched a few cross marks all around. To an onlooker, it did look like an excellent army position plan.

Etash lied in his bed contemplating whether it was too early? How did it work exactly? If he thought about Inu and went there, would it mean she would be there?. Or she would be there in her own time and convenience, and it will have to be a coincidence to be there at the same time that she was.

Nevertheless, he would never know if he did not go, right?

This time, it was almost immediate.

The corridor was a familiar place by now. Etash did not want to enter the door that he had last time, lest he ran into The Buffalo again. "Oh **Paramaatma, NO!**", he thought.

He was now confused. He wished he knew behind which door Inu was. He decided to try his luck and knock on one of the doors. He just remembered it had to be two knocks.

And there was that feeling again. As if being watched. Being followed. Etash turned back, there was just a blanket in a corner. He tried to calm his jittery nerves. He slowly went ahead and knocked twice on one of the doors.

A smart looking woman opened the door. Etash was disappointed, it wasn't 'her.'

The woman invited him in. He saw what seemed like a party. People hanging out, talking, laughing, and generally being happy. He had not been to a party ever. He was an introvert. Partying was not his scene. Off late, however, he felt the need to improve his social skills.

He now walked into a room full of people.

"There he is! Everybody, please give him a warm welcome", the voice said.

"Oh! No! No! No! , he started thinking, but before he could confirm his doubt, everyone turned around and gave him loud applause.

Amidst the sound of the applause, Etash stood wondering, "He is everywhere! Is The Buffalo an important 'person?' in this whole scheme of things.

He felt a light press on his shoulder. "It's tough!", said the old lady as he turned around. "I had a difficult first time too!!", After being perplexed for a moment, he understood she was talking about being introduced to this group of people.

"Well, well, well! , I am sure you did not expect me here!"

The Buffalo kept talking as he continued walking towards Etash.

"I was expecting you, but I was hoping not," said Etash trying to be nasty.

"Were you hoping it would be me instead," said a melodic voice behind him. The voice that gave him goosebumps, every single time he heard.

Inu slid her hand into his and led him to a corner. This was the first time he had felt her touch. He felt a jitter running through his body. He just followed her, captivated by her green eyes. He did not care where they were going. He was jolted back when he tripped on something. It was a stairway. "This wasn't here before," he thought absently.

He did not care enough to discuss the details. He just wanted to go wherever Inu took him.

Etash and Inu in a candid moment...

The stairway ended at a colonial door. It had what seemed like handcrafted floral carvings that looked beautiful. Inu creaked opened the door to an unbelievable visual that Etash could not even begin to describe at that moment. It was space!

She slowly led him into space. He half expected a fall, but the other half that had seen enough science fiction thrillers was not surprised when they floated.

This seemed like King Kakudmi's travel in the Sanskrit novel he often read.

"Can I talk.." He tried conversing to distract his mind off the steep fall below, above and all around him!

"Don't worry, you will get answers to all your questions. However, this will take several days. I will gently lead you to it" Inu said.

As they floated around, he noticed shapes like palaces, beautiful dancing ladies and Kings go past in a blur. "Was he in some sort of heaven?"

Then he saw a big gate ahead. The entrance was in between clouds. As they approached the entrance, it opened up. They slowly glided into a corridor made of clouds. He could hear loud conversations. The corridor suddenly opened into a huge meeting room.

Inu spoke. "You favorite man, The Professor, has invited us to this important meeting. Though you may not realize yet, you are an essential member of this team."

"I guess, I must congratulation myself," thought Etash.

They sat at the end of the table and tried to listen to what seemed like a leader giving instructions.

The Professor was saying - "This is a very very critical moment for us. We need to plan very well and be very agile about everything. Etash here has some interesting thoughts. He has a long history. Of course, he hasn't had a self-realization trip yet. In the coming few days Inu will support Etash to realize himself. I feel, if he realizes his true potential, he can grow to lead us from the front." The Professor now turned towards Etash "You have a lot of work to do. Inu will accompany you and support you until you are completely enlightened and ready to be part of this great team. Rest of the nitty-gritty we shall go ahead and plan. You guys carry on. You and Inu probably would want to explore the multiverse a bit. So we will leave you to it. All the best!"

Inu gently led him out of the conference room, back to the cloudy corridor and into space again.

"Do you want to see anything in particular?" asked Inu. "Do you want to see how the time can be stored maybe? Or the cloud storage devices we have or maybe the expanding multiverse.."

The look on Etash's face made her stop. He looked like he had had enough for the day.

She said "It's ok. We have a lot of time to understand the whole thing. Let us go back now."

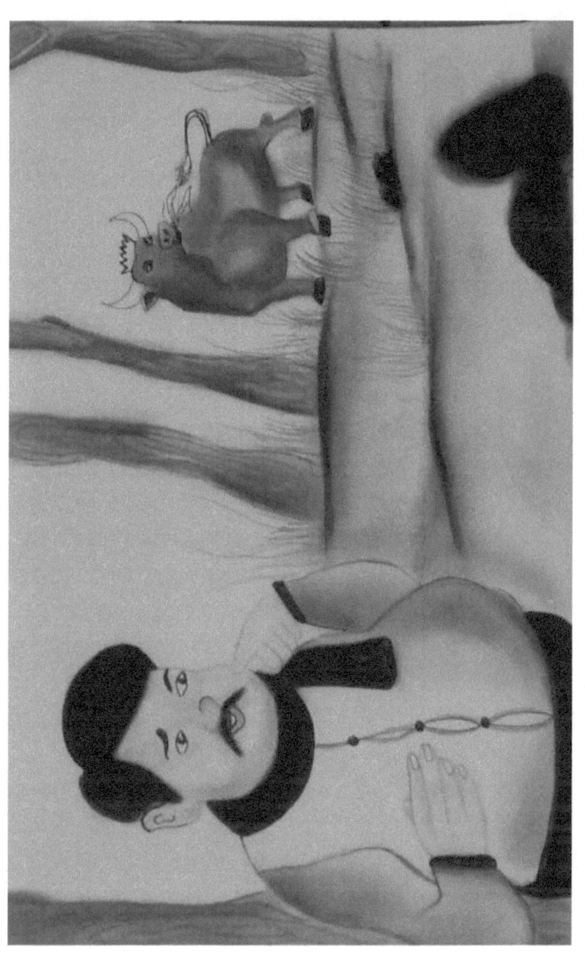

Chair-man observing the Buffalo with suspicion – "We just ate the last of buffaloes last week. This is a no buffalo land. Where did this come from?"

Chapter 8

Buffaloes have the talent to be present in multiple universes at the same time. You can make that out from their laziness. They aren't really lazy. It's the transitioning effect of their presence in the multiverse that gives such an effect.

The buffalo stood there chewing – nothing - as usual. This was not a buffalo country. They had long ago, eaten up all their buffaloes. No!, there were no other possibilities. The people just loved buffalo meat in these parts, especially the ribs!
To an innocent passer-by, the buffalo seemed utterly uninterested in the events around.
The Chair-man was one of the intelligent ones though. He quickly understood that this was a weird incident, spotting a buffalo in this country. After all, he got the chair as a recognition of his intelligence. He still remembered his Guru's words "Man! This is an important assignment. The king is not very intelligent. We, from the Gurukul, have complete faith in you. Use your intelligence and plot to make the king, an emperor. All the best."

He observed the movement of the buffalo's eyes. seemed to be uninterested. He saw the tail, and swatted indifferently as well.

"Hmm, acting smart is it?!!' The Chair-man thought.
"Namaskar!", He said, and joined his hands above the head, watching the buffalo, cautiously, stepping back one-step-at-a-time.

After reaching a safe distance away from the buffalo, he fled the scene in an instant.

Seeing this, the buffalo disappeared.

For the same innocent passer-by as earlier, this would have looked like an aberration, like it was something he imagined.

The Chair-man heaved a sigh of relief on reaching his office. His manager, his constant companion, was already in the cabin. He quickly sat down and started sketching feverishly.

"Do you think it will work? The wall does look impressive already", The companion Asked a little bit tensed.

"Meh!, I am the greatest plotter of wars. This is simple. All we need is, to attack from here, and then from there, and here, and there! Simple!" he said in self-assurance. It is said that doubts and ideas float around in the sky looking for sufficiently empty brains. The Chair-man scratched his head. He suddenly felt doubtful. He tried not to show his concern in front of his manager. Not that his manager would have noticed. The manager was still having some of the last of the chicken masalas.

As he looked at the wall, The Chair-man had a tick. Usually, people have waves in their brain.

The Chair-man's brain would not survive a wave, a tick was sufficiently draining for him

"We need a change. Plotting on the wall is very common. We need to get a proper plan. We should probably start creating presentations on a computer. That would be visually alluring."

"This is all the time travel there is," Inu said. "So now we are partners."

As they slowly came back into the familiar corridor outside Inu's thought room, he had that jittery feeling again. He looked at Inu.

"Do not look back. Just hold my hand and follow me" Inu almost whispered. She held his hand tight and got into a sprint. She opened the door to the right and went in pulling him behind her. There seemed to be a party going on there too. "Again a party?!!" she looked at him and said in an exasperated tone. She pulled him to a side and there she led them through another door. It was another party. Then the door, then another party, then corridor and then through the tunnel, woosh and they were back in his room.

Etash did what any brave man with enough self-realization would do in a situation like his. He gave Inu complete control. "What next?" Etash had given himself up. Inu did not reply. She just smiled.

Inu waved at him as she disappeared.

It was all darkness again. Except for the faint comforting glow of the street light flowing in through the window. Etash slowly closed his eyes as deep sleep engulfed him.

"Thud, splatter, crash" Etash woke up with a startle. It took a minute for his brain to take stock of him. One head, two hands, two legs. Slowly he became aware of himself. He was back in his room. It was still dark outside. The room was locked. The sound must have been from his neighbor's house.

He got up and picked up the jug on the side table. It was empty. He remembered having filled it up before going to sleep. As he went to the kitchen, he noticed the floor. It was as if 10 days of dust had accumulated. He usually cleaned his room every day!

A casual glance at the clock shocked him. It was 9 o'clock!! He had slept at 9 o'clock. "So everything had happened in a blur!!" he was shocked.

A closer look at the clock gave him the answer. It was a Saturday!! He had slept on a Wednesday!! "That's three whole days!!! What about my body? Who took care of my body? I do not feel that hungry or weak." He thought to himself.

He got hold of his mobile and dialed the number.

"I need The Professor. I need urgent help! I need urgent help" he muttered to himself.

There was no response from the other side

"Yes, the only option is…" He made up his mind. He went to the bedroom.

He started dressing up as a man with determination. Totally focused. One could almost hear the background music of "Heroes is forever." Almost felt like a Superman wearing his costume.

The ring of the doorbell brought him back. No, It did not shock him. He had had enough shocks for a lifetime. 9 Clock was not an unearthly hour. He could have visitors.

As he opened the door, he heard the now familiar " You slept enough already. I thought of waking you up, but then my mother taught me to never wake up a sleeping man. Will you let me in? It's so cold outside!!"

Yes, this time there were no surprises. It was Inu outside.

"Hey you are ready," she said on seeing him. "Great let us go and have dinner."

He pulled the door shut and walked with her in silence. He had submitted to her as far as he remembered his dream adventure.

As they walked in silence through the dark pathway to the pizza place, he did not feel like asking any questions. This usually happens in a marriage. A man may go out with friends on a trekking trip. They may share their sad marriage stories. But once they return, all that matters is one is back home.

It was just enough that Inu was walking with him. The pizza place was empty today. They were the only customers.

They sat down waiting for their order. Inu began" ok, I am sure you would have a lot of questions in your mind. We have a method to introduce a new person to the world of truth. So that the person gets enough time to settle down well. I am allowed to tell you some things now, so let us see where do I start?"

"Why don't you start from the dark path, that place where I suddenly got sucked. The womb thingy."

"That would be a good start. We did that to get you acquainted with the risks involved in such travels and make you gain control on your navigations. Sorry, I was not allowed to help you there. It was your struggle in the womb. Consider it as your rebirth. You need to learn the art of controlled entry into the thought world. "

"Where is The Professor?" asked Etash, just as Inu finished talking.

"That is another interesting question too. However, remember that usually knowledge doesn't work like that. You start with A for apple. We are a group of people with knowledge on entry into thought world, or you may call it Thought Dimension. I prefer Thought Dimension as it gives a more accurate picture of its existence. It is beyond being a world. It is even beyond being a universe. So, welcome to the group" She held his hand and shook it. "Professor would probably explain to you further about the group, whenever you meet him. So that's all I can tell about The Professor right now. What else would you want to know?" She looked at him and raised her eyebrow in question.

"Who is following me? Whom did we escape from in the thought world..sorry.Thought Dimension the other day?"

"We are under some big siege. I'm not completely informed. The Professor can explain this as well. There are some souls called *Patali*. They are from *Patali*. They seem to be making some plans to attack various dimensions of the multiverse. They seem to be making appearances everywhere. They are following me as well. The Professor has warned about them and instructed us to try and escape, erasing our track. I haven't had as many instances of them following me as you. They seem to be taking an extra special interest in you. Do be careful" She held his hand and pressed it gently. She looked him in the eye and continued" Have you heard about matter transmission?"

"As I said earlier, you are using the power of Positrons to push your soul cells up. You are observing your soul cells and guiding them to the crown and beyond. You can call it, self-realization. By observing and focusing one can move the soul cells towards self-realization. In your case, it is spontaneous, though. You still haven't grasped the art of controlled movement."

"I think I am getting the drift of this conversation. So you're saying that I can control the position of my soul. Right?"

"To an extent, Yes. Don't get too excited. You have a long way to go."

"Hey wait, what if.."

"You are right ...it is possible...If moving of the positrons of the souls is not done in a controlled manner, one can end up damaged or totally disintegrated. It becomes very messy then. Our group usually tries to salvage such souls. However, if we don't find them on time, souls can get lost and wander off. You are fine with the technology. You are safe. Don't worry. You are well monitored."

"I hope so" Etash sighed.

"what?!!!"

"....we are almost near donkey now."

"what?!!!"

"Ha ha! , we started with A for Apple, and we have reached, D for donkey! , get it?" , she gestured pointing her index finger on her forehead.

He simply smiled.

She held his unresisting hands and led him out into the cold breeze.

Chapter 9

The Chair-man had to start working on the powerpoint presentation. But he wasn't sure about what was needed. He had to find a way. There should be something written somewhere. He had approached the nearest library and asked for a book on 'How to fix the writing on the wall?' or 'The war in words.' He did not get any help from the librarian. He had tried the internet and checked on the famous search engine "mind-boggle.com." Finally, as a last resort, he took his management studies book and glanced through the chapters.

Suddenly he recalled. "I almost forgot my dear friend -The Web-man. I can depend on him. He has been in the thick of web since time immemorial. I'm sure he can get me out of this mess. That boy of his, Yuvan, his wall did seem very interesting. Let me ask The Web-man if I can get Yuvan here."

He punched in some numbers on his phone right away.

"Hey, webby-cobby. How are you? Listen, I'm in a mess. Can you spin a web for me? I have to strategize a war, and I wrote it on a wall. But the font and the color are not impressive. I need to get something done quickly. The situation is like this, psst...pssst. We need somebody who can strategize a war and create a powerpoint presentation of it."

He heard a muffled voice from the other side as if coming through a lot of layers of web. "Yes, I have the right person for you. I have a star-boy."
Before The Web-man could continue, The Chair-man interrupted "Yes, of course, you have a brilliant idea. However, just a small suggestion. What if we have Yuvan here instead of the star-boy?"

"Oh yes, that was a good idea. Very brilliant I must say. Just a small change though. How about we have the star-boy, instead of Yuvan?" said The Web-man more assertively this time.

This healthy professional discussion went on for a while.
"Ok, in that case, it is your risk. Let us try with Yuvan", agreed with The Web-man, at last.
The Chair-man looked quite happy now. The Web-man seemed to have a solution to almost any problem.

At the other end, the Web-man was clearly unhappy.
"The Chair-man is questioning me! This is not done! I'm running this organization for 20 years now. He wants Yuvan, he gets Yuvan. But I do the planning here!" he thought. There was thunder and a bolt of lightning. He turned and smiled. He could still remember his first introduction to Yuvan. His boss had spoken to him about the issue "See man, we have this person who has been good at his job. Though I hand him over to you as a team member, he would be more of a peer to you, due to his capabilities. Utilize his skills well, and you can get great results". The Web-man had been hurt by

that. He didn't need anybody's support. From that day on, The Web-man had tried to bring down Yuvan in front of his boss.

"I'm the boss. I own the team. Who is Yuvan? From day one he has questioned my authority. I brought him here to humiliate him. Now, this Chair-man has somehow got fooled by his charm. He wants a powerpoint presentation, and he is asking for a person with wall skills!!" thought The Web-man.

"You be safe. Do not venture into the thought world much" she seemed worried.

"What's worrying you?" Etash asked.

"I have to leave for a while. There is an urgent and important thing I need to attend to. I'm worried about your navigation in the thought world. Ok, I will tell you one important secret, a way to communicate through the thoughts without actually going into thought world. When you are focusing your thoughts, your energy, to go into the thought world...at a point of an increased level of awareness, if you stop and then focus on the souls near you, you will find some souls vibrating in sync with you. They are your friends. Just communicate with them and tell the end recipient's name - mine. The message will travel through the network and reach me. It is not safe from hacking, but at least for emergencies and for normal discussions, it should be ok. Keep your wooden box handy when you travel. Also, watch out for *Patali* souls." Inu held his hand tight as she spoke. She then turned and left.

He felt all alone suddenly. Of course, he was alone in the house. But this was different. It was almost equal to the feeling of a child left in school for the first time by the parent. He went in and tried to focus on the TV.

Several eyes were observing him. They slowly diverted their attention towards each other. They were in a big conference hall. One of them, with some of the eyes among the ones observing Etash, spoke "We *Patali* have to win this time. Let us focus on all the key elements of this group. We should be aware of their plans in advance. I'm so far happy with your progress. You have monitored him well. Try to follow his movements closely so that you can hear him. Sitting here in *Patali* and observing him is sheer laziness."

The others listened intently. The One seemed to be the leader. The one continued "Now, as an induction into the *Patali* warrior clan, let me introduce you to our organizational structure. I am the head of the *Patali* warrior clan. You can call me The Professor. I will soon appoint some of you as leads. We all report into a group called the PSI, the *Patali* Intelligence Service. Hmm, coming to think of it, for some reason the order of abbreviation is not PIS! I hope you all understand this robust structure well. It is important during the war to be aware of the escalation matrix. I will send a copy of this structure, to you. Any questions?"

The rest of the *Patali* had lost interest in the conversation. They had each drifted off. There is a saying among the *Patali* "An average *Patali* warrior is either asleep or in a war."

Chapter 10

The Web-man walked in with his usual gait.

"Hey, You have been doing a great job! It's awesome to see you while working", he said.

Yuvan was startled. He turned around to make sure it was actually The Web-man speaking!

"I have an awesome opportunity for you, my man! I just got off a call with the most amazing man. He is looking for a warrior with multiple skillsets. Someone who can create a PowerPoint presentation too! I suggested your name. I wanted to give you the best possible break. I think this will do you wonders!"

Yuvan just listened, 'after all, right now, I'm in oblivion. What can go wrong? In the worst case, this will turn out to be a dud', he thought.

"Do I confirm it then? I see you are excited. Ok, get packing. This opportunity is in the kingdom. I'm sure you will have a great time", The Web-man seemed more excited for Yuvan, than he was for himself.

Yuvan remembered the last time he got a 'great opportunity' when he ended up being in the line of fire for the, well, ironically enough, the fire accident! Then there was this other 'great opportunity' that had become a nightmare with extended work hours and unearthly hour calls and blame game. He had then decided: Nirvana. He needed the oblivion. He had had enough of whatever was being played against him. "All I wanted was some recognition." he had thought in dismay.

It is written-one cannot think straight when one's bladder is full.

Inu was in a similar situation_ Etash seemed to fill her thoughts_ she just could not concentrate on her job. She was supposed to crack the location of a secret manuscript, but her bladder was actually full now.

As she attended to nature's call, she attended to the other one, one from The Professor - both calls of duty.

"What's happening Inu? You seem to be losing it."

"No sir, I'm completely on it. I'm heading to Joisaji's house. I will find it soon. I will also find the guy. It will all go as planned."

"Ok, it is important that you find that artefact, the ancient writing, the hidden gem. I just got an update that it will be in the form of writings on a leaf. The owner of the house in which you find it will also have the ability to read it. Remember, it is an important Mantra. We need it for the war. Needless to say, make sure that the *Patali* don't find you."

"Yes, sir. You can trust me. However, the last map you provided me seems a bit weird. 'Take the first left at the dead-end!?"

"That's just to distract the *Patali*. They get confused very easily. They go by the grammar and would take ages to understand instructions like that."

Inu hung up. She still remembered the meeting. The Professor had called her and told "Inu, there is important ancient writing, 'secret art of fighting the *Patali*.' It is somewhere to the south of this place. We have an approximate direction on this map. Please rush and find it. We will take care of Etash till then. I will send The Buffalo to get him." She had been a little bit angry at this. She had just started the process of inducting Etash into the group.

She had also just begun the process of understanding her feelings towards Etash. Suddenly to be sent on another mission was irksome. But no one questioned The Professor in the group. He was the ultimate authority.

The Professor on the other side seemed worried. He was thinking,"Distracting Inu seems like a good idea. We need to keep Etash on his toes until we are able to succeed in our mission. Inu seems to be calming Etash down. He may soon lose interest. Of course, the mission Inu is given is very important as well. According to the sources, there is a possibility that the great artefact 'secret art of fighting the *Patali*,' is still not destroyed. Oh, *Paramatma*, please forgive me for misleading this young girl."

Chapter 11

Yuvan is pacing up and down, in his mind. These days, he did not have the motivation to pace up and down physically. The Web-man was missing since their last discussion. He had merely spoken to him about this great assignment and asked him to pack. He wanted to discuss and get some assurances and support from The Web-man. It looked like that was not to be.

His phone rang. It was The Chair-man.

"Hey, my best workman! I hope you are ready. You are going to have an awesome time in the kingdom. I will take care of you. We will complement each other. You take care of the presentation; I will take care of the rest. You take care of the ideas; I will take care of the rest. You convince the councilors, and the king, I will take care of the rest."

"Was it five 'rests,' or was it six?" Yuvan tried to distract himself from this obvious shenanigan.

He started running now... he was getting desperate to meet The Professor. A few minutes back he was watching TV at home. He had tried to relax and divert his attention from all the thought dimension business. However, Inu's departure had unnerved him. He had started running towards the professor's house without a thought. It was as if he was not in control of himself.

The steps leading to his house were very steep or maybe he was weaker, and he needed to exercise.

To his disappointment, the house was locked. Dejected, he walked down the stairs and came to an auto-rickshaw stand. As he was about to hail an auto-rickshaw somebody tapped on his shoulder.

He turned and looking at the person who had tapped he made his ears burn hot! "What?!!!!" One's voice shows one's emotions. His was extruding irritation. It is said that at the other end of extreme anger is extreme calmness. That's not true! At the other end of extreme anger is............ still just extreme anger.

"I'm supposed to take you to the place of knowledge." said The Buffalo.

"What?!!!" Etash was still agitated to think correctly.

"You don't seem smart. **Paramaatma** knows what all the hype is about!"

"You are the...", muttered Etash, completely confused. It seemed weird. This buffalo keeps following him. It was fine in the thought dimension or in dreams. Strange things happen there. But here? In real life?!!

"Where do you want to take me?"

"We don't have time. I hope you have had a bath."

"What?!!! And this coming from a buffalo.!!"

"The next bus is in an hour. Let us take an auto-rickshaw to the bus stop, and we should be on time."

He stood there baffled! There was nothing to discuss. The fat man seemed to have a persuasive voice he could not ignore. "What?!! The fat man? How did...?? Where did??", he seemed to be asking questions to himself. What was happening!! And

then he noticed the fat man chewing, he had stark
similarities.

Chapter 12

Yuvan climbed onto his chariot. The Chair-man seemed to be powerful. Usually, they gave a bullock cart for his grade employees. He was given a chariot! It seemed unimportant at this point that the chariot was driven by a bullock.

He sat at the back and started reading through the book collection on the history of war. He was trying to assess a pattern in the victories.

The books were handed to him by The Web-man as he embarked upon his journey.

The Web-man had told him, "I'm always there to help you. I have protected you these many years. Take these books. They may help you."

"Maybe this is the great opportunity after all." Yuvan thought "The Web-man seems to have understood me finally."

The bus ride was tolerable. He slightly moved his eyeballs to the left to glance at the stout man. He wanted to avoid any conversation with him. The stout man seemed like he was dead! Was he meditating? Etash decided not to bother himself by asking any questions.

"I hate it when these young beauties call me fat!!"

"What?!!"

"Oh, my *Paramaatma*!! Again with the "what?"! Do you even know other words? I really hope you are not as dumb as you look and sound. And I really really hope Inu has not made her first mistake. She is a smart girl. How on earth did you manage to impress her?"

"What?!!!"

This time The Buffalo did not even acknowledge the 'what?'.

He woke up when it started feeling hot. The bus had come to a halt, and the cold breeze that hit his face on the moving bus had come to a stop too. He never thought about it, but he always fell asleep in a moving bus, ever since he could remember.

He got down and looked around for the stout Man. There was no sign of him. He started to worry a little. As annoying as The Buffalo was, Etash had begun to enjoy his company. The banter was entertaining. The Buffalo was witty. He gazed across the road, his eyes searching for The Buffalo. He felt comforted with the visual. The Buffalo was grazing peacefully in the green patch across the street. As he moved ahead to cross the street, he was startled by a loud horn of a truck. He stepped back and turned around angrily to yell at the driver. It was not a shock anymore. The Buffalo was standing at the back of a truck. It had hired the truck for the rest of their journey!

Chapter 13

The Star-boy had been looking out through his window. As soon as Yuvan's chariot went out of sight, he turned towards The Web-man and asked "so he is already off. When do you think your plan will work? After he becomes the king?"

Web-man with his protégé "The Star-boy"

The Web-man explained to the Star-boy very patiently, as a father explains to his son "don't worry. Just believe in me. Blah.blah.Blah"
The Star-boy was all excited on hearing the idea. He clapped his hands like a kid who had found candies, a lot of them.
The Star-boy thought "Aah! Finally, my time has arrived. I'm the best. I have to rule the universe. The Web-man is in my control. He is pretty dumb. I'm sure I can outwit that dumb Chair-man as well.

Etash was dreaming about a comfortable bed with warm lighting and the soothing breeze of a slow moving fan when the truck bumped big on a pothole. Etash opened his eyes when The buffalo's swatting tail hit his face.

The Buffalo seemed to be enjoying. It had the smirk on it.

"So you like this form?" Etash tried to converse.

"Gruuuunnnnnnnnnntttttttt"

"Stop grunting! You are in human form. Stop embarrassing me!"

"Gruuuunnnnnnnnnntttttttt"

"Arghhh! , why do I even try?" thought Etash, furious. He thought it was better to just close his eyes for a while. Not long enough, he was in his thought world.

Etash was glad to be there. "What do we have here? This door looks good. Etash kept moving.

"Gruuuunnnnnnnnnntttttttt. I know you won't knock. You don't like me do you?" came The Buffalo's voice.

"What is there not to like you. You smell good. You have a beautiful voice." Etash said as he opened the door. It was a nice, cozy shed. There was hay everywhere. There was dampness. The dung was all collected and kept in a corner. "Hmm, you have some interiors here!"

"Gruuuunnnnnnnnnntttttttt, I guess you were not taught to be good for animals. Anyways, we have a lot of work tomorrow. I hope you wake up rested and polite."

"Where are you taking me?"

"To a secret place. You are some kind of genius who has to do something. I can't see what is possible for you to be honest. I mean with all politeness and all due respect and all."

"I will let that pass. Where is Inu? Didn't she send you? You are related to The Professor as well aren't you?"

"Well we are all related, aren't we? In some way or another. You really need to sleep now." The Buffalo just knocked him down with its horns.

Chapter 14

It was getting dark. Yuvan had come a long way to a town. He decided to stay in a nearby Inn for the night. He bought sufficient hay for the buffalo and went into the room. Soon a shriek was heard. Yuvan ran out of the room in his bathrobe. He was furious. He went to the reception and started yelling, "I was promised hot water! There is no hot water. It's icy cold. How can I have a bath."

The receptionist spoke calmly, "Sir; we have a strict policy against usage of hot water for a bath. In fact, we have a strict policy against having a bath on days other than Tuesdays."

"You say hot water available, Yuvan pointed at a board behind her, "right there!"

"Sir, we meant hot water is available for drinking."

"You haven't mentioned that there! I will go to the consumer forum. I will take you to the highest echelons of the law."

"Sir, would you like to cancel your room? We can gladly help you check out right now."

"Hold on, hold on. Everybody calm down." It was a woman's voice. He turned around to the sight of a young woman behind him.

"You don't go out much, do you? A very pampered kid..huh? Now keep quiet and let me do the talking." , she said.

She turned towards the receptionist and asked, "So, you provide hot water for drinking only. Can you send the water to the room please."

The receptionist nodded.

"Ok, send five buckets of hot water to the room please."

"Mam, bucket?!!"

> "Yes, I drink a lot. Any problem?" she turned towards Yuvan and held his hand "Come now, the receptionist is kind enough to send us the hot drinking water to the room quickly, I can see it." Yuvan followed the girl to his room, as if in a trance.

The Professor of *Patali* was in a meeting.

"Oh, the esteemed PSI. I have a great war-plan. Please look at this presentation."

An Intelligent Officer stood up. Every member of PSI had the title of Intelligent Officer. The Professor of *Patali* stopped and folded his hand in reverence.

"This is great! All this font, color and the images you have used. We would like you to personally oversee the war. Keep giving us the status. We don't mind attending a status meeting every hour."

The *Patali* Professor bowed. The meeting was over. As he stepped out his assistant looked curiously towards him.

The *Patali* professor smiled "PSI likes wars. They like wars on humans. The usage of red colors in our presentation did the trick. They like to paint red. If given a chance they would paint the universe blood red. We have the budget for the war. We just need to get hold of that boy, Etash. Judging by the importance he is being given by the human Professor, I'm sure he is the most important person in his scheme of things. We kidnap Etash, and the professor is doomed." The *Patali* professor's smile had a know-it-all attitude. After all, he knew it all. He

knew the human Professor like the back of his hand.
This time, it seemed like his time.

Chapter 15

The Web-man was sitting by a window. He was taking deep puffs of his cigarette and thinking, "Yuvan has to be brought down on his knees. He is nothing but trouble. Even when sitting in oblivion, he keeps making noise. I need to obliterate him!"

The history between The Web-man and Yuvan went a long way back. It was so very long way back that even history didn't have much track of the events. As far as The Web-man remembers, it all started when…… or maybe it started when…… it is difficult to remember. The Web-man was very sure of one thing. The inner seething rage against Yuvan.

Thunder and lightning follow. The bolt hits The Web-man's face and burns down his cigarette. He turns and sees his reflection in the mirror on the wall. Then he turns to the window and smiles. He picks up his famous-brand-of-the-rich phone, dials a number, and speaks "Have you reached your destination?"

A voice from the phone "Yes, I just had a bath. We are waiting for dinner."

"Great, gain his trust. You need to be able to stall Yuvan. Will send you the plans soon."

The Girl sat on the bed thinking. The Web-man had called her a few days back. "There is an important assignment that suits your status as a secret agent. We have one warrior heading towards The Kingdom. He is smart and is developing some strategy to overthrow the king. Stall him. I'm arranging to warn the king. Stall him until then."

A fresh day, a fresh beginning

It didn't seem so fresh though.

They had reached a ghost town at about 10pm. Etash vaguely remembered being woken up by The Buffalo and being shown into a hut by a river bank. He had just dropped into the hay arranged as a bed and slept like a log. The stress of the previous few days and the long travel had taken a toll on his physical and emotional well-being.

As he was in an early morning slumber, half-awake, The Buffalo entered the room.

"So you are awake, baby boy? Gruuuunnnnnnnnnnttttttt"

"Will you always be around!!"

"It is a new day sweetie, calls for new habits. Why don't you brush your teeth for a change? Gruuuunnnnnnnnnttttttt"

"And why don't you bathe for a change?"

"Gruuuunnnnnnnnnttttttt!! Gruuuunnnnnnnnnttttttt!! You got a mouth on you don't you?" The Buffalo said.

Etash did not want to get into another banter. "What is the plan? Why am I here? What is happening?" he asked trying to change the mood.

"If you will be so good as to brush your teeth and freshen up then we can have breakfast. You can go to the river. Later there will be a lot of answers waiting for you. Oh my dear dumb one, Gruuuunnnnnnnnnttttttt."

In about an hour, they were below a Banyan tree having breakfast. The Buffalo was having idly. In between the chomp chomps, The Buffalo spoke "Your sweetheart is on her way back from some research. She may take another couple of days."

"My sweetheart?!"

"Yes, I know you can't think of anything but Inu. But we have a lot of work to do. To begin with, you need some answers. (Slurp) This sambar is awesome. (Slurp) You are delicate but very valuable. People may want to destroy you. Hence all the secrecy while bringing you here. Here we are guarded and safe for now. (Slurp) Do you know about the (Slurp) balance of the universe? (Slurp) The universe is balanced with good and bad."

"You mean 'bad' is a plan by the universe?"

"You can put it like that. However, it has to be balanced with good. It is this rule written somewhere and to cut the story short, the balance is at stake now. The bad is winning.

"You cut the story very short. It almost made no sense."

"OK! Let me elaborate. Every time balance of the universe is at stake the *Paramaatma*, the supreme Shakti, the *Parabrahma* has to balance it back by coming to the universe in physical form – the avatar. It is like creating a power to attract everything to itself. The universe as you know is ever expanding. In fact, the multiverse is ever expanding. Stories are taking up multiple alternate options. Thoughts are being corrupted. The multiverse is going out of control."

"I am trying to understand, and?"

"You cannot grasp the magnitude of this in one discussion. You are currently not aware of your strengths. Or so they say. I would say you have no strength ... Anyways... You need to visit the training center now...brrrrrr... Gruuuunnnnnnnnnnttttttt."

"Buffaloes burp?.!"

"Do you want me to show you everything buffaloes can do?", The buffalo was now annoyed.

Chapter 16

> "You are a scientist?"
> "Yes"
> "And you want to go to the kingdom to study the habits of the king's family. I am sorry, did I hear it right? You want to study them - to understand why they all have a pot belly!"
> "Yes! Pretty much."
> Yuvan was speaking to the girl as he loaded his stuff onto his chariot. The buffalo had just had his fill of hay and was ready.
> "And what did you say your name was?"
> "I'm Isha."
> The name sounded familiar to Yuvan. He thought for a moment. But then he wanted to get going. He had read a few more chapters from his books and had some ideas that he wanted to write down.

"Mix one quarter of vodka and two bottles of gin. Now what you have is a pretty tasteless shit!!"

Inu was sitting in a bar. To an informed eye like a shady bar on some Highway. Not everyone is informed though.

She was nearing the Joisa's house. She had traveled a lot of distance over the past few days. Every time she got to a proper point to enter the Josia's house, she would notice a *Patali* nearby, and she had to call The Professor for a quick exit from there. This time she had made sure the point was not well watched. She had to just get drunk and act like a drunk. She could then easily give the slip to whoever was looking out for an intelligent and smart looking girl. She looked around to see if she was being watched. Everything seemed normal around. Except for the people standing at the bar counter. Were they quadruplets or something?!! All of them looked similar. "Well, there can be seven people like each other in the world. But all of them at one bar counter?!!"

The patrons, as well as the bar attendant, had not noticed her as a girl, let alone a beautiful girl. The mind sometimes just believes what isn't there, rather than the apparent fantasy of truth. How can a beautiful girl be alone in this dark bar!! It can't be right. Of course, her using a manly voice had also helped.

She slowly slipped out of the bar and walked towards the Joisa's house. As she had correctly guessed, nobody noticed her. A few of the *Patali* wandering nearby ignored her. A beautiful drunk girl, walking haphazardly, in shabby clothes, is usually the imagination of a desperate mind. People generally ignored such visions. *Patali* was no exception to this general principle of human behavior. After all, *Patali* souls had evolved learning from Humans.

The house was beautiful. It was definitely several centuries old. It seemed to be made from mud. At least from outside, it looked tiny. She slowly went to the back. As an experienced group member, she knew the tricks of the trade. One should check the escape routes before barging in. It seemed like an area of washing vessels, with a small tank and a few stone slabs around. There was a small entrance to the house at the back. The door was open. She thought of knocking on the door and then felt the better off it, lest she awakens a stray *Patali* nearby.

She walked in, making sure she checked everything as she did so.

The inner house surprised her. What should have been a max of a fifteen-foot area, turned out to be huge. It was bigger than any building she had ever seen. She turned back to make sure the door was still open. To her shock, she could not see any. She seemed to have entered a maze.

Realization dawned on her that she could not just walk in and then walk out. She had to awaken herself. Breathing in and out she slowly got into the mode. Anulom Vilom was the way – the breathing technique of inhaling with one nostril and exhaling with the other. As the cells raised, through the Sushumna and then the crown, she started to get a view of the place. She had entered a universe of its own. It was too huge for her to start looking around. She focused on vibrations nearby. She could feel it pretty close. She headed in the direction through the eyes of faith and there she saw him, a man clad in a saffron robe. He sat there meditating, with an ever knowing smile on his face. "He must be Joisa." she thought.

Waking up a soul who is on a journey in the multiverse is never a great idea. She sat in front of him and waited.

Pretty soon, in a matter of time, the man opened his eyes. Of course, in such a dimension it would be difficult to calculate the time.

"The message you seek is here. In the hands of a strong soul, this can be a savior of the universe. Give this to no one but Etash. You give it to anyone else and "Joisa took a deep breath. It looked like he was about to say something awful. Inu could make out by the way Joisa had stopped in between is a sentence. Joisa continued, "If at all you give it to anyone else nothing much will happen. Nobody can understand the message other than Etash."

She took the leaf with the message on it. It was crystal clear. There was no encryption. Joisa seemed to have arranged for her to be able to understand it.

She looked at Joisa for further instructions. Joisa smiled knowingly "The Professor has the good intention at heart. He is misleading Etash and you to attract someone. He has some big ideas. Anyways, remember that Only Etash should read this leaf. All the very best on your future endeavors."

Then suddenly everything disappeared in a flash. Inu found herself in a potato field. She was confident it was a potato farm. There was the distinct smell of the manure.

Chapter 17

The Chair-man is sweating. It was a tough day. He had to wade off questions from councilors.

"How much money did you spend on the wall?"

"Did you read the writing on the wall before presenting it?"

"Why should we believe this new power point presentation of yours would help change the way we plan wars?"

The Chair-man stood up and cleared his throat.

"Gentlemen, ladies. I understand your concerns. The wall has been the approach for designing our wars and presenting our proclamations. We stand by our decision to create our most important plan, 'the war of wars,' on the wall. However, do you all not agree that I should bring to you whenever new innovations are available? Shouldn't our kingdom be as tech-savvy as our neighbors? I do not ask for all your budget at once, my dear councilors. I just ask for a meager few billions. When you see the output of my work, I'm sure you will give me more."

The councilors were thrown off track by this speech. They were not sure what it meant. They would have to discuss with their assistants. "Meagre few billions"- he said. We can't be shown to be worried about something meager." They thought.

A man with a pot belly and a pot-head stood up to speak "You have very well laid out your plans. We shall analyze this in detail and get back to you. "

The Chair-man stood with a smile. He knew his next steps.

This fully functional hospital stood in a ghost town!

The Buffalo had changed into a more comfortable form. It was now a buffalo that can crouch. Very important for walking on the tiled floor of the hospital.

Did it just wink? Did The Buffalo just wink at the nurse?!!!!

"Are you a ..You know ...she Buffalo or a he-buffalo?" Etash could not control his curiosity.

"You can't make that out, can you? And you are supposed to be our hero!!!!

They entered what seemed like an ordinary hospital ward – a little unconventional though. The sheets were not white. They were colorful bedsheets with a sober design. The patients looked like they were on vacation.

"Where are we? What is this place?"

"Ok. Sit down and make yourself comfortable. Professor will be here soon.

"Professor?!!"

"Yes, He is the boss! He knows everything - and beyond."

"Hello there, my boy!, I have been waiting for you!" The Professor came closer and gave Etash a warm hug.

"Let us go to the control room. Let me start by showing you something and then I can clarify your doubts." The Professor led them to the nursing station outside the ward. "Our control room" he announced dramatically.

There were several chairs scattered around. And one small led TV. There was a USB stick attached to the TV. And there was a keyboard.

"That keyboard is for your benefit. You are in a new body, and sometimes the brain cells of the body override the soul. Sit, let me give you some recap. You are a reincarnation. You are a powerful soldier in the personal army of the three powers of the multiverse. You have been taking birth as a sage, as a mighty help to the **Paramaatma** during several wars against evil, as a prime minister of a powerful country during World war…..and many more. Also, remember! All these across the multiverse."

"I have had several reincarnations. I'm a powerful person. I'm here for a purpose too. I have got this power to control my soul cells and move out of the body. I can even enter this Thought Dimension, which of course, seems to be a portal onto something else." Etash slowly said as if recapping what had been told to him so far.

"Very well summarised. Now some science. There is a part of the body in your lower spine called Sacral Plexus. It is triangular in form. The spinal cord can be represented by an '8' piled one on top of other above the Sacral Plexus. The Sacral Plexus is the lotus of *Kundalini*. The left of the '8' is Ida and right is Pingala. A very narrow canal that runs through the center of the '8' is the Sushumna. There is a lot of potential energy at the base in the lotus. This is the energy of the Atma or self. People practice various forms of Yoga to awaken this energy through Muladhara, through *Nadi* and reach *Sahasrara*. The point when the awakening has reached the crown or *Sahasrara* is the epitome of awakening within the body. For most people, that is the maximum energy one can handle. Getting this energy to the level that you push your awareness of self, beyond the crown, now that's something you have been doing. Let us call it the power of push. There is a power of pull as well. The power of pull can usually mean death, or maybe someone has summoned you for a discussion. The power of push is what you and many of us have inherently. It allows us to get into Thought Dimension. Sometimes people do realize this power in sleep inadvertently. But very rarely remember it when they wake up. So far so good?"

Etash nodded "Just one thing though. Where is the science in this? This seems to be out of the *Puranas*." he was kind of getting the 'hang' of where this was headed. He had always thought that quantum theory, with *Puranas* and *Vedas*, could explain the mystery of the universe.

Professor ignored his question and continued, "Going deeper into this concept, any cell - every atom, kind of, has a representation of the *Paramaatma* in them. This Power connects all of us. You can find me where you seek me. As you know, positrons can be seen where you see them. You cannot exactly predict their position, but you can see them with the power of a true seeker."

"I hope you are not taking the unknown in science and mixing it with religion to somehow convince yourself of something. "

The Professor again ignored his comment. "The positrons in common person would be bound by the cell. So within the bounds of the cell, its position can be observed. The Positrons can be used to push the cells around. This requires a lot of focus. With this approach, you can take your soul cells out of your body, for a walk around the multiverse!!! And if you take all the cells for a walk, you are physically moving into the Thought Dimension!! As you have been doing for a few days now."

"Quantum travel explained. Inu did explain this a bit. You explained it further." Etash still had some doubts. "Ok. So Inu…"

"Yes, she travels with her physical body into thought world. She says it feels safer that way. We all can do that - travel either with physical body or without it. It is just the next stage of self-awareness. It is all the same: Quantum travel, Thought Dimension travel, *Kundalini* awakening, matter transmission_ at the end of it, we have some unique power. We have to use it for the good of others."

"Hmm…"

"Now look at the TV screen. Do you see a mass of red moving in? That is the one we are worried about - the influence of *Patali* on the universe or multiverse as you may want to call it. The patches of green - that's us the humans. Now if you see closely, It is all balanced. There are as many greens as reds. The universe works on balance. Why are we worried?" A long pause to dramatize his speech. The Professor was always a professor in whatever dimension he was operational.

"The grey bits. That's what we are here for."

"I think I understand what you mean. Everybody has good and bad in them. But *Patali* are tilting the balance in favor of the bad, Seeping into the good and affecting the balance."

"Yes!! Awesome, see I told you. I have seen his brilliance during the World war-his previous birth."

The Buffalo just grimaced.

Chapter 18

"Stop! Stop right there.", said a loud husky voice. The buffalo stopped as if it understood.
Yuvan and Isha looked around scared. The buffalo- just looked. So far it is not very clear what a scared buffalo looks like. A wide-eyed buffalo lifting its tail does look scared. The buffalo in question did not seem wide-eyed.
A short man approached them from behind a large boulder. He had the attire of a bandit. "I'm the official bandit of this area." He announced.
"Official?!" asked a puzzled Yuvan.
"Yes, in these parts we take legality very seriously. We only deal with legal people. I'm very serious about the legality of my work. You are witnessing a professional transaction. So please handover 1/3rd of the valuables you are carrying."
"He..hee, haa" Yuvan could not control his laughter. The short man didn't even seem to have a proper weapon. "Let me try and see where you are. I can't even see you clearly from this height." Yuvan got down from his chariot. Isha was looking at the proceedings very curiously. She suddenly became alert and stood up.
"Yeah yaa hooo. Ye yep." the short man got into a martial arts stance.
Yuvan stood confused. The stance caught him unawares.
Isha jumped down to his side. Cautiously she held Yuvan's arm and started pulling him towards the chariot.
"Yeah hoooo."

Isha had pulled Yuvan back behind the buffalo. The buffalo was looking at the short man with interest, as he seemed to be getting ready for a powerful attack. Seeing his manoeuvres sent a chill down Yuvan's spine. Isha seemed to be shivering a little too.

Next few moments went in a blur. The short man jumped towards them, and then the buffalo pounced towards the short man. There was a lot of punches, kicks, and shrieks. It all stopped as quickly as it started. There was absolute silence. Yuvan looked to his side. Isha was still there. He looked at the chariot. It was there too. He looked at the buffalo. It seemed to be there, tied to the chariot. Was that a smirk on its face?!!

The short man was nowhere to be seen.

They gathered their composure and slowly set off on their further journey towards the kingdom. Yuvan noted down somethings he had noticed. "Hmm!! Interesting. Hee hooo. Yeee haaa. I hope I got the spells proper," he thought.

"Ok, I'm drunk. I'm supposed to walk like a drunk" Inu slowly got up.

She stepped out of the bar. She had entered a random bar after coming out of the potato field. She just needed something to get out of the intensity of the Joisa incident.

As she struggled to walk, she thought "Shouldn't someone try to rob me? Then I fight, get hit. That's how it went in that movie. With the tall hero. That time he got hit, he seemed to reach a state of bliss and dozed off." She was thinking of random thoughts.

"Meine Nahi pee..zamana hai kharab..." inebriated, she crooned a tune vaguely remembering the lyrics.

As it goes with nature sometimes, you think of it, and it happens. Someone stopped her from behind. She stopped; she thought she knew exactly what she needed to do. "Now for a roundhouse kick. Wait, I have to be hurt first."

The man seemed to get cold feet. He could feel that this was a girl. A drunk girl. It was midnight. They were just outside a roadside bar. Didn't seem right. He just ran away even before she could request him to hit her.

"I need to get some sleep in a nice bed. I can't think straight." She felt comfort at the thought that the message on the leaf was safe in her backpack.

A group of *Patali* folks was still at the bar. They had noticed her going in and followed. Looking at the girl drink, they had copied. The temptation of copying human behavior was irresistible to a *Patali*. The Alcohol had knocked them off cold though. A *Patali* warrior's brain is not advanced. A *Patali* warrior doesn't need much of it. The rush of blood to the brain after alcohol was too much to handle.

Chapter 19

"Something weird is happening here." It was from Isha. She was speaking on her phone. "Everyday of our journey we are being attacked by weird beings. There seems to be some pattern to it. "
It was a conference call.
The Chair-man was in the call too. "Look here. I have managed the councilors for now. I need Yuvan here as soon as possible. I need a proper war plan, in a powerpoint format with proper colors. I hope you understand the magnitude of the problem here."
"Hmmm, I understand both of you," said The Web-man. "Isha, it is essential that Yuvan focus on creating the plan. I had given him some documents. It has all the details. Get him to read the books and synthesize his thoughts. We have to avoid any disturbances in his work. Do change your course and move through the eastern highway. There would be lesser chances of bandits there."
"As you say, sir. If I may, I think this incident helped trigger some ideas in Yuvan. I saw him scribbling things in his book."
"Ha, a book. What good will it do? We need color full presentation. What good will he learn from looking at a fight? He should be rather studying the art from the books I have given him. Make sure he is reading them." The Web-man told haughtily. He did not show his emotion though.
"Yes, get him to complete his notes."

"This is surreal," Etash thought to himself.

Usually, there were about 50,000 people in the hall – asleep - their souls in the thought world. They were the Professor's army. Regular maintenance of the cloud was their duty, now that Inu was busy in the other task. With some urgent keystrokes on his keyboard, the Professor had invoked all the souls to be present in the great hall. Right now, they were right in front of Etash and were looking at him with reverence. The professor spoke to them in a deep voice "This is Etash, the greatest power we have been waiting for. He will lead us to victory. It is going to be a famous victory. We should all feel proud to be part of the great event that is unfolding. Even to be able to see him here is sufficient strength for us. Do remember him in your hearts and go on and continue to do your duty."

The Professor's army seemed all charged up. They brimmed with hatred for the *Patali*. Each of them had had a horrible personal experience with the *Patali*. They had waited for an opportunity to avenge all the ills the *Patali* had subjected them to. Looking at the very person whom the Professor had described as the supreme power who would help them, defeat the *Patali* had infused a deep self-belief in them. One could feel the power of this belief in the air. Etash almost felt like he was being lifted off his feet with this power.

The Professor dismissed the army back to their work. They walked back into the inner chamber with the computers in it. Etash for the first time noticed a small temple at the back of the chamber. There were idols and photos of his favorite gods there. The Professor asked him to sit in front of the temple, and himself sat beside him. They sat in silence for a few minutes.

"Slowly close your eyes. Breath slow. Focus on the area at the bottom of your spine. Do you feel anything?" The Professor's voice was slow and deep.

"Yeah! Like something from somewhere deep is trying to go everywhere. Is that ...gas!?" his voice sounded 'a matter of fact.' Etash was not trained in the art of social conversations. These were biological activities, and he was quite practical about it.

The Buffalo sniggered from somewhere nearby.

"Those are your soul cells! You need to control the Positrons within them. Now try to focus a little above. Slowly moving up. Let the cells follow you. Not too fast."

"Haven't I already done this?" He wasn't sure what The Professor was aiming to achieve here.

"Yes, but that was more of a sub-conscious thing. I want you to control this. We have a lot to achieve. The future of the multiverse depends on you. Please focus." The Professor had a sense of urgency in his tone.

They were in the corner of the ward now practicing the art of controlling the soul cells, and of course, it's movement outside the body.

"Now, as you near the base of the neck you may stop hearing me and become totally focused. That's when I will also start my journey into the Thought Dimension and join you there."

"Hmm..." Etash muttered absent-mindedly.

"The Buffalo, of course, has his own way. We can be sure to meet him there."

The tunnel appeared. Etash had come to the thought world completely controlled!!

As he crossed the tunnel, he noticed he was back into the hospital. However, he could see himself now.

"Yes, with control, the Thought Dimension need not just look like out of your imagination. Right now, although you are in Thought Dimension, you are in the present, on earth, looking at yourself. The space that looks like out of your imagination is still available, as a portal into the multiverse at large." The Professor was explaining, beside him, in the Thought Dimension.

"Hmm, where is the portal?"

"Follow me."

The Professor and Etash went towards the east. Slowly heading out of the hospital. Rising as they moved, Up, Up. Now they were moving slowly towards the East. As they walked there, ahead, he saw a new tunnel.

"Ok, this is like a hole in ozone or a portal." Etash could not control the excitement in his voice.

"Once you are out, you are beyond time. Out of the universe as you know today."

"This is where Inu brought me earlier, But..."

"Yes, she made it look like a flight of stairs. You can imagine it to be anything that gives you comfort. Since we are out of time-space paradigm, taking stock of time as in the universe would be difficult. You can enter the universe back at any time. To be back at the same time, we have to trace back our steps exactly. Which is difficult. So don't be shocked if we lose a few days."

"Lose?? As in - 'time' can be lost?!"

"Well, haven't you had instances where you have felt it was just Friday yesterday and it is already Monday?"

"Well, I thought it was a theory of relativity. Anyways, return to the same time? You mean back to the tunnel, back to the hospital? We can bookmark the time?"

"Not that easy. When you go back to the portal and look close, you will find layers of it. Multiple universes, Multiverse if you may. Every moment a new possibility gives birth to a new universe. To enter back into the same universe with possibilities of your choice is the challenge. These days we have created a predictor using a technology called Slark. We can approximately trace back or reverse-predict which universe is the one you left behind. You can focus on the tunnel in the portal. The scenes on its led panel-They give you an idea of the universe. You can fairly make a choice from it. Of course, you must focus on a more proper channel, not some stupid Bollywood dance."

"But last time it seemed very simple."

"Yes, you were simply guided by one of our members each time. Last time of course by Inu. She is an expert and has a profound knowledge of the process. She has maintained our cloud for a long time now."

"Can we go back now? My physical body needs some food." said the Buffalo

Back at the hospital, someone had arranged a sumptuous meal.

"You seem to have a lot of budget." Etash was trying to understand the magnitude of what The Professor was running here.

"Well, the King of money is with us. Now relax for the day. You have learned the art of controlled matter transmission. Next, we need to be able to split. Let us relax for now." The Professor tried to calm Etash down.

Etash heard what sounded like thunder. It was getting dark outside.

Chapter 20

"Slurp"

"Chruuup"

They were clearly enjoying their coffee. The Chairman though seemed to be calculating. He had planned this meeting with some of the advisors of the councilors.

"Billions are spent every year on the modernization of the flag post on the fort. I'm sure it is important, psychologically. , However, I would like to draw your attention to this report, which shows the number of wars won just by solid, lucid presentations? Just look at the graph. Think what a good presentation depicting our strength can do. It would help us build an aura that we are invincible." He spoke as the advisors continued focusing on their coffee.

One of the advisors spoke "Let us not get into very deeper topics. Flag post is a matter of historical importance to the kingdom. You are a newcomer. Please do not get into something that would push you in dangerous waters. This coffee is awesome though."

The Chairman tried to lighten up the mood "yes, of course. Ha.hahhaa. I just remembered a joke. Once a man tried to climb a flagpole_."

An old advisor interrupted him. He started coughing loudly before he spoke "I'm sure we are all very mature here. We can manage a flag post and also try and see what comes out of the presentation this gentleman refers to. I assume one of you will accompany The Chair-man to the fest in the garden tonight. It is going to be fine."

"We need a gap. Keep observing the entrances and exits to the town. Are you sure about your information? Is Etash in that town?" The professor of *Patali* was asking his team. They had come closer to earth. He had brought a few trusted lieutenants along. He was trying to find Etash. He could not have delegated this task. He had to do it himself.

"He followed the buffalo into the town. We are not able to enter the town. We can barely see movements in the town. Something is blocking our physical entry" an assistant replied.

"That's the special subnet cover that The Professor of humans has placed. We can't even hear what people speak inside. Just monitor the movements. Keep me informed when Etash comes out and follow him. We need to learn the entire plan before we kidnap him."

The Professor of *Patali* applied some oil on his several eyes. He had learned this from humans. One's eyes do not get tired if oil is used.

Chapter 21

They had reached a river. According to the map, they had to cross it. Isha was trying desperately to contact a boatsman. Nobody seemed interested. Yuvan was busy with his books. Isha had adviced him to focus on his work and leave the planning to her. The buffalo was happily grazing in a field nearby.

"Ma'am, it is getting dark. We won't get passengers on the return journey. It will cost double."

"Ma'am, this is peak hour. A lot of current in that direction. It is dangerous. It will cost four times."

"Ma'am, your chariot has four wheels. It will cost you four times."

"Ma'am, I'm bored of rowing. It will cost you ten times."

Initially, Isha had let them all go in confidence that someone will agree. Now the bank was empty. All boatmen had left with other passengers. Now it was getting dark.

An old man had been watching them with interest. He approached them now. "So you want to cross? I can help you."

"How do you plan to help? You don't seem to have a boat."

The old man laughed and threw away his shawl. He showed his palm and said, "You get your chariot ready. Let me take care of the rest."

Then things happened in a blur. Yuvan looked at the proceedings with interest. The old man seemed to be rotating very fast. He entered the river as Yuvan watched in amaze. His palms moved in lightning speed now. He was cutting the current using his palm and making an area of dry land in between. The Buffalo followed pulling the chariot behind. Every time the driver tried to make a new opening for it to flow, the old man's palm would come in that place. He was cutting off the supply. Within a few minutes, they had crossed the river.

Yuvan looked at himself. He wasn't wet. He looked at Isha; she wasn't wet either. He looked at the buffalo. One could not make out from its slimy skin. He looked for the old man. He had disappeared!!

"The army believes in you. I have immense belief in you. You need to start believing in yourself. We will help you in your quest for self-realization. Listen, take the next bus to Mangalapura and then from there to Kanyagad, a place will give you a clear idea of your present birth. The Buffalo will accompany you. By the by, Mr. Buffalo sir, please, you can't go there in your current shape. You can't even get on a bus as a buffalo. Maybe a young stud type man would be a good shape. I'm getting a strong signal for the presence of *Patali* folks. So be careful." the professor gave specific instructions to his companions.

"Gruuuunnnnnnnnnntttttt ...." The Buffalo seemed unhappy.

They headed out of the hospital. Towards the end of the road, from the circle next to the hospital, they found the bus stop. The Buffalo had decided the form he wanted to take - An old man with no teeth!!

"I understand matter transmission, rebirth, etc. But how do you change shapes?" Etash did not expect a proper answer. He just wanted to make a conversation.

And expectedly, The Buffalo answered in its usual smutty way "I will tell you a short story. Once upon a time, there was a boy. He asked The Buffalo the secret of changing forms. The Buffalo did not tell. Do you like the story? Now sleep..."

"Why are you rude?"

"You stop being an idiot, I will stop being rude."

The bus started its journey on the winding road through Bhagavati forest.

"Baby boy, that there, is the birthplace of Bhadra river. We shall try and visit that place on our way back."

"Ok, where are we going?"

"Let me tell you a short story. Once a boy wanted to know where he was going. The Buffalo told him that it is more important to know where he is coming from. Do you like it?"

Etash shook his head and kept moving.

A man covered in bedsheet was sitting behind them. A few people covered in bedsheet were seated in the front row just behind the driver. A few people covered in bedsheet were sitting at the back. It was a freezing winter day. Wearing a bedsheet as protection was typical for the town's folks.

After a few minutes of travel, The Buffalo covered itself and Etash with a bedsheet.

Chapter 22

"Hmm! Interesting. Palm, to stop the flow."

Yuvan started scribbling in his book. He was getting several ideas at once now.
Isha had an urge to call The Chair-man and give status. Something stopped her. The look in Yuvan's eyes as he scribbled ferociously. He looked like a super excited toddler using a drawing pencil.

She remembered her conversation with the Web-man. "Yuvan has this problem in his brain. Though he works well in synthesizing data and is good at strategizing, he usually drifts. He gets dangerous ideas."

The Web-man had paused to observe Isha's expression before continuing.
"Yuvan, He could be a threat to the kingdom. Observe him carefully. Stall him you must. Also, any work that he produces should be handed over to a friend in the kingdom, star-boy. The Chair-man, I understand you have worked with him earlier. Keep giving him the status of your journey. Just add that Yuvan has delayed your travel. Just trust me and do it."

Isha was feeling a hereto-unknown emotion. She had thought of nothing on the Web-man's command then. However, the past few days with Yuvan had softened her.

She thought 'I don't want to mess this boy's life. He

Inu needed a way of reaching out to Etash. Maybe the professor could help.

She quickly pulled out her mobile and dialed The Professor. "Sir, I have got the message. Mr.Joisa informed that this was made for the eyes of the true warriors. He says only Etash can decipher the message."

The Professor thought "Why would Joisa insist about showing the message to Etash only?. She probably wants to meet Etash. She must be missing him. Etash is nearing the end of his mission. He would soon attract 'the person,' and we would be complete. There is no harm in letting them meet. Even if she shows him the message, there is no harm."

He replied on the call "That's fine Inu. You will need to go to Kanyagad. There, near the fort on the beach, you will meet The Buffalo. He will take you to Etash."

Inu was a bit disappointed. There were other ways of transporting herself which were faster. The Professor seemed to be trying to stall her.

Chapter 23

Did I mess it up? Should I not have asked for Yuvan specifically? Should I have let The Web-man assign someone? At least someone would have been accountable! It is more than a month since Yuvan started his travel to the kingdom. How do I finish the presentation?' The Chair-man was thinking.

He took his mobile phone and speed dialed The Web-man.

"Hey Webby-Cobby, no sign of our boy, *Paramatma*! I'm worried. I have taken a lot of trouble, worked really hard and spent a lot of time convincing the advisors to the councilors. We have the necessary budget. But we don't have him yet! Where is he?"

The Web-man could not let go off of this opportunity.

"Well, what can I say? He is your boy. You chose him. Ok, let us do one thing. Let us get our Star-boy to travel as well. You say you have a budget. Let us not waste the budget." , he said sarcastically.

"Let me think about it. I will have to build a case for the requirement of a second person to make a presentation." , the Chair-man was now worried.

"Maybe you can send Yuvan back. After all, he is late." , suggested the Web-man as shrewd as he could get.

'Particles can themselves be teleported. Sometimes some cells have something called Quantum entanglement – sharing of quantum states by particles. The cells do not need to belong to the same body or the same entity. The quantum entanglement may happen to cells far off.'

Etash was reading some notes he found in The Professor's desk.

He thought "First the Thought Dimension, then quantum travel, communication through similar cells with common vibrations, matter transmission, *Kundalini* awakening and now Quantum teleportation. Do all these meet somewhere? Are these people trying to have their soul positrons travel to different parts and then communicate with each other from there? Is it equivalent to growing as huge as the universe and then being able to look around, something that Lord Krishna did several centuries ago? What are they trying to look around for? What is this bad that is winning? Who are *Patali*?"

The sudden honk of the bus woke him up or rather got him out of the train of thoughts. He wasn't in The Professor's room! Had he traveled there through the Thought Dimension?!! He was covered in a bedsheet and sitting very close to the old man who was The Buffalo.

"Interesting angle of thoughts you have...I can see why people are giving you so much importance" The Buffalo whispered.

"Can you trust me enough to tell me more, please? This suspense is killing..."

"It was once told....never trust your water when the bus is full of people."

"Did you tell that?"

"All I can say is, going to where we are going will bring you enough enlightenment to realize your potential. Additionally, you may get to relish some popular food items."

The bus was slowly coming into a large bus stop.

"We need to get down now. Let us quickly have lunch and then take the next available cab heading towards Kanyangad." The Buffalo was still whispering.

"Finally, we are heading towards some destination!! " Etash was getting annoyed by all the secrecy and whispers.

Ignoring the sarcasm in his voice, The Buffalo now shaped as an Old Man got up.

The bus stop was busy with several private buses.

As they got down The Old Man started looking at a group of young girls standing nearby. The girls caught him drooling and teasingly said, "Hey Grandpa, how are you!!...."

"I don't mind the giggles, but then, they call me grandpa ??"

"Why do you have to take the form of an old man? I thought you could take the form of whatever that you wished to be...." Etash sounded exasperated. The Buffalo was getting on his nerves.

"Rules kiddo! Rules! The universe is what it is, because of the rules. Even the bad follow the rules of the universe. So what would you want to try? Some red boiled rice with dark fried chilly? Maybe it would prep up your mind to understand your origins."

As they left the bus stand, a few persons sitting at the back of the bus, woke up. They seemed to yawn. It was difficult to make out the facial features within the bedsheets they had covered themselves with. They slowly stood up and looked shocked. Again, the shocked expression could only be imagined based on their body movements. They had lost sight of essential targets. As people who were in for some severe reprimand from their boss, they vanished with drooped shoulders.

The Buffalo and Etash thought of having lunch. After a simple but delicious meal in a restaurant run at a house, called by locals as a 'Mess,' they got into a taxi. Well, the old man got into it. Etash was left hanging outside holding onto his dear life!!

Chapter 24

"Haiiyaaa hooo hooo….. Hoooo Haiyaa Hoooo…."
The sound woke him up. He tried to move his hands and realized that he was tied up. It was pitch dark. He was not familiar with the surrounding. It felt like he was in the water.
 "Ouch!" It was boiling water.

Suddenly there were more sounds. "Pataaarrrrrrr!!!!" something came crashing, and it was bright now. It took a while for his eyes get light-adapted. A large number of people dressed strangely running away from a bear. The bear was walking with confidence. It was not growling. It was not confusing. It was walking straight at the strange men. This frightened the men thought they were armed to the teeth. Something walking with a purpose surely would know what it wants to do. They did not want to find out.

He was sitting tied up in a cauldron. Somebody had tried cooking him!!
"Hey, let me help you" Isha came up and started untying him."That bear came out of nowhere and helped us. I could hardly move."

Yuvan got onto his feet slowly and stepped out of the cauldron. He looked in the direction of the strange people. They had disappeared. He looked at Isha. She was still there. He looked ahead. His chariot was there. The buffalo was tied to it and seemed very comfortable standing there. The bear had disappeared.

Soon they were on their way. It seemed like something very routine very mundane happened, and it was as if nothing happened. It was a pattern. Yuvan started noting down "Confident stance and a sense of purpose."

As Inu sat in the train towards Mangalapuram, she had a train of thought running in her mind. Quiet faster than the actual train that she was sitting in....

The day when she was introduced to the club. She had by then been to the Thought Dimension a few times. She had always taken her physical body with her, unlike Etash. It is all about matter transmission, she knew. Etash had been too quantum about the travels.

And then she had met The Buffalo, the guardian of the Thought Dimension. The Buffalo as she learned later had been a loyal companion to The King of Death. In the era of Kaliyug, the universe was getting difficult to be balanced, and The Buffalo had taken up the duty of keeping a watch on anything that spoils the balance. The idea is to save the good souls ...that's what The Buffalo had explained to her one day.

Someone, somewhere suddenly starts believing that they can take over the entire multiverse. It is always the same. Someone gets some power, and then they want to rule. Usually with great power, one gets a great ego, it is a package deal. This time it was the *Patali*. But the multiverse still had a way to restore balance.

The concepts were pretty vague she had thought. It is beyond anybody within the universe to understand this_The Buffalo had explained.

And then the shocker…she was the daughter of the time.

As the beautiful forests of the Ghat passed by, she felt relaxed. She could feel her soul cells near the crown of the neck. She felt bad about herself for having indulged in drinks. "The multiverse is so pleasant. One could be in the highest state of bliss with this *Kundalini* awakening. The drinks just messed up everything" she thought to herself.

She felt the urge to try the Quantum Entanglement approach to communicate with Etash.

"Let me try it now," thought Inu

"Adi, are you awake? Can you hear me?"

The message seemed to just be there in her mind as if it was echoing within her and then…

"Why do you call me Adi? I don't like that."

"Well, that is your name isn't it?"

"I prefer Etash."

"ok, Etash…so you are in Kanyangad now?"

"Yes, just got down from the taxi. Horrible experience that, I am unable to feel any part of the body anymore."

"Oh, you have achieved the first stage of learning matter transmission to transmit your body then!!"

"Are we really in a conversation? I thought this was some kind of a hobby of my mind..you know..talking to itself…but you do sound like you now."

"Looks like at some atomic level we have got into quantum entanglement! Somehow our souls are able to communicate with each other!!"

 "Gruuuunnnnnnnnttttttt ….."

"Ok, The Buffalo can tune into our conversation too!"

"Is there somehow to end the conversation or is it just we focus on something else?!"

"Let me focus on catching some sleep then, see you soon."

Chapter 25

The Star-boy had arrived.

"War is about having a proper framework. We need to enhance our security. Every chariot should have soldiers around. We should have a few soldiers on top of the chariot. Everything is about security."

The Chair-man had received the Star-boy at the border of the kingdom on his arrival and was taking him to his residence. He was pretty impressed with his thoughts.

"It would make sense. Security in a war. That's novel.", he thought.

"We have prepared several delicacies for you. We have made some bitter gourd sweet, bitter gourd curd, bitter gourd pulav" The Chairman wanted to make the Star-boy happy.

"What?!!"

"Bit.."

"Bit what?!! Let me manage my dinner, please. Do not take trouble" The Star-boy was apparently not impressed.

Inu woke up with a jerk. She kept her eyes closed. She had been trained for such situations. Her sixth sense cried danger. Opening her eyes would alert whoever the danger is from.

She put all her focus onto the sounds around her. There was the sound of a chugging train. Somebody seemed to be snoring in the next seat. As she started gaining awareness, her consciousness started slowly moving beyond her body. She was aware of her body lying down on the seat of the train. She started seeking the source of her fear. At first, she ignored the corner and started looking ahead. Her mind pulled her back to the corner. "There, that must be it," she thought to herself. In the corner huddled to each other were a few bed sheets. Probably there were a few occupants in it.

She decided it was time for some quick action. Lifting her consciousness further she elevated her mind to a layer above. After a layer of deep darkness, there it was. The deep connectivity layer of thoughts. She quickly transmitted alert signals to friendly souls nearby, who would, in turn, transmit the thoughts to The Professor, through multiple layers of friendly souls.

"I need to be teleported" She whispered.

It took a while for the network to reach its destination. It took more than a while. Inu started getting restless. "Professor, come on. We need to hurry" she thought to herself.

And then she received the message "The network has been activated for your teleportation. The strategic units for the multi-step transmission are ready. It is risky. Take care"

She knew that it was risky. Multi-step teleportation involved moving the body and souls through the thoughts of multiple friendly souls one soul at a time. The chances of cells getting mixed up and getting lost were very high. Such risky maneuvers were only for such urgent situations as the current one.

Chapter 26

They sat looking at the scarlet sunset.

Isha had slowly opened up. "I think we are being manipulated. I can't see why you would be considered a poor performer! You have great ideas. And I'm a strategist. What am I doing here?"

Yuvan thought hard. "You are right. This mission does not make any sense. I can't see why the Web-man would provide me with an opportunity so good!"

"No, hold on. Don't be demotivated. I think we can find our purpose. You have made a document. I saw you scribbling all through the way."

Yuvan slowly handed out his book. Isha glanced through some pages.

"This can be a big treasure," she said thrilled. "If we take this to the king, he may recognize your worth."

Yuvan nodded. "Yes, let us go. Let us find this kingdom."

"How many people were they in total?" The *Patali* Professor was fuming.

"Two, sir" his assistants replied.

"And how many were you?"

"Four! Sir!"

"And you could still not follow them? You entirely lost track of where they went?!!"

"Sir!"

"And now what do you expect me to do? Congratulate you?"

"Sir!"

"Idiots. Bunch of idiots. Ok, let us watch the entrance to the ghost township closely. I'm sure they will come back." As the assistants went out of his office, the *Patali* Professor quickly dialed a number on his hotline facility. The nametag on the phone displayed 'PSI Head' prominently.

"Sir, I'm focused on the job. We have corrupted 1,034,500 souls in the universe.

The voice on the other side was stern "Good. Keep up the good job. Do you have a corrupted leader we can rely on?"

"We are trying sir. We are focusing on a link called Etash. He seems to be their strength. If we cannot corrupt him, we kidnap him and use as a bargaining chip. It is all well planned, sir."

"Hmm, a strong person from the enemy can be converted into a weak link. Awesome concept, professor. Do keep me posted."

Meanwhile, Inu was being teleported to the beach near Kanyangad. She was physically transmitted through friendly souls stationed at convenient distances.

As she jumped into the dimension of the next soul, she met a handsome man. They did not have time for a proper conversation though.

The handsome man just passed on a message. "Nice to meet you and all that. Next jump would be to a lady near the fort. She will provide you further instructions."

"Hmm, boring people! Where did The Professor get hold of them?" she thought as she had a chance to quickly look at the rural village which was the Thought Dimension of this person and then whoosh. She was in another Thought Dimension.

"Hey, how are you dear? Heard a lot about you. I'm a big fan" the lady seemed middle aged. The Thought Dimension was now a forest clearing.

"I probably need to jump quickly. The *Patali* are pretty close." She was tele-conversing with The Professor now.

"Yes, The Professor explained. However, the jump from the man to me has been massive already. You are nearing the zone. You can't jump anymore. If we eject now, we would be able to land close to the island."

"Oh!! The legendary island. I get to see it finally is it?" she said to herself.

The middle-aged lady gently held her hand and led her into a bathroom.

"A bathroom?!!", she thought. Everyone had his or her own type of exits. Etash had a tunnel. She preferred a pathway with signs 'Ausgang' it had a very rustic feel to it.

The waves!! What did she do to make them so angry? They were lashing at her.

The woman left her hand and said, "The Buffalo will be here soon. Once you reach the island, all traces would be washed off. You can then be back on your quest. All the best." the woman walked off to the parking lot of the fort.

"Gruuuunnnnnnnnntttttttt"

"You are my guide for today, are you?"

"Gruuuunnnnnnnnntttttttt"

"I understand. I'm ready."

In a few minutes, they set off on the journey to the unknown island.

"I didn't say I was ready to snuggle near you..!"

"Ha Ha…that's the beauty of this journey."

"And what makes you want to talk, pray!?"

"Gruuuunnnnnnnnntttttttt …"

"Understood."

Chapter 27

Her phone kept ringing. Isha looked at Yuvan. He nodded his head. Isha picked up and answered, "Hello!"

"What's happening Isha? No status for some time. Did Yuvan prepare the presentation? We have a great resource at our disposal now, the Star-boy! He will modify the presentation with some of his great ideas. We need to give the presentation to the Star-boy. He will need the basics from Yuvan." the Web-man was losing patience.
"We are almost at the kingdom. We will hand over the presentation to the king directly. Yuvan seems to have done a good job."
"Wait, Isha, that's not your mission. You need to handover to the Star-boy. Listen...Listen. Can you hear me? "

"Beep...beep" the phone disconnected.

The Professor seemed like an anxious man. He was frowning as he looked at his computer. The darkness of the *Patali* souls was now very dense around the universe. They were slowly taking over all galaxies from what he saw in the report.

Each of the galaxies, each Positron, was providing data to the data processing unit on the cloud. The amount of data being processed by their cloud was more significant than anything that could be even thought of as significant. It was a new technology they had come up with and named 'Muzoop' –

physical soul cells that transmitted and processed each other's data as a cluster.

He slowly turned from his chair towards the people on the bed. Some of them were awake, others in deep slumber. He addressed them as if they all were assembled for his speech and were attentive.

"The souls from *Patali* are slowly taking over all the known universe. They have spread across as we feared. Additionally, with the corruption of some good souls, they are able to become denser now. This is nothing like before. None of the previous wars can match this. Let us keep our training focused. Let us be prepared for the war to bring balance to the universe."

He then thought for a while. " The last war had been a disaster. While the balance had been restored finally, the **Paramaatma** themselves had to come to the aid of the universe. He had an inkling that if let be, even the current one may go that way. The only way was to get 'the man' on board. The guy along with The Buffalo would be a great frontal attack. Getting 'the man' to come out of his island was the most significant task ever, and the right person for the job seemed like his son.

"Let us see how things turn out." he thought to himself.

The plan seemed to foolproof. Split ourselves into several Positrons, split ourselves across the universe, fight the battle everywhere and never spread out thin.

However, what were the *Patali* folks up to? They seemed to have a plan up their sleeves as well. He knew The *Patali* Professor well. They had played together as children. That was several centuries ago. They had fought several wars against each other as well.

In deep thought, The Professor kept walking around a circle in front of the hospital. The Professor was walking in circles, thinking in circles.

Chapter 28

The chariot was going at a decent speed. At least from a buffalo's perspective. The road had started getting busy. It was almost dawn. Several morning walkers looked at the chariot as they walked ahead. They were in the kingdom. They were clear about the path forward. Of course, the kingdom was prosperous and had clear pathways, but that had nothing to do with their clarity.

As they reached near the border, Isha called The Chair-man on his mobile. "Sir, we are here."

The Chair-man did not sound very excited "Oh! I almost forgot. I have arranged accommodation for you in the Sanghvi apartments. I have informed the security. He will give you the keys to your rooms. Take some rest. You can come by to my office tomorrow."

She turned towards Yuvan "Things have started playing out already. We need to plant our story soon. The Chair-man has already lost interest in you."

The chariot moved towards Sanghvi apartments. Isha knew the kingdom well. The buffalo pulled on.

"People don't tell me anything. They all seem to have a strategy. They act as if they know everything. They somehow need me. I'm supposed to be a hero in waiting, a person with a mission. I just have to realize my potential. Really?!!!" Etash was lost in his thoughts sitting alone on a rocky cliff.

"Yeah, it has been a tough last few days. Don't even mention it. I hate this travel." Agreed Inu

"Gruuuunnnnnnnntttttt"

"Ok, things do happen very fast, and there is always the fifth element waiting to happen," Etash thought to himself as he turned to face Inu and The Buffalo, all in their original shapes.

"Today we can relax. We go tomorrow to meet the king. Gruuuunnnnnnnnntttttt"

"Alright!" Etash had given up. It was pointless asking anything. The only thought that came into his mind every now and then as if all this was necessary? Did he need to get involved? What was his role? Was there any way he could have avoided being in this situation?

The Buffalo headed downhill, he probably had some important meeting to attend, or maybe something that only buffaloes may consider necessary.

"So, did you miss me?"

Etash smiled in reluctant acceptance.

"It was great fun going around shady areas and drinking. I was supposed to meet this man called Joisa. I had a gala time. If only you were there."

"Why were you drinking?"

Inu brought him up to speed on the plans of The Professor and her role.

"Hmm, interesting! You know what I think? I think The Professor is having it all wrong. I can feel it. I can't point my finger at it yet though."

"What? How do you mean?", Inu did not know how to react to this thought.

"Well, for one, I think I know my role. Not the role The Professor is planning for me, the real one. I can tell you more once I analyze some of the historical data. Then I need to take stock of the current facts. From there it should be easy to understand why we are under attack? What is the end goal? , and maybe find an escape strategy!"

"Hmm. Ok. We can do all that. I can help you. But right now you have to read this. I have got hold of this message. It is from Joisa. I have been asked to show it to you first."

Etash took the box containing the leaf with the message. He slowly opened it. There was a flash of light. As he slowing picked it up, the entire surrounding started glowing. And then a small head popped out. It looked like a little monkey's head. It started speaking. "Since eternity people try to find hidden messages all over. People end up ignoring visible messages. You and Inu, you both should analyze what you already know. Head to the cloud. Everything will become clear there," and then everything went dark. When a sudden bright light goes off the eyes take time to adjust. Etash was trying to adjust his eyes. Inu had already grasped the gist. "Let's go," she said and held his hand.

Chapter 29

"Why do I need this man now? I thought we discussed that the Star-boy was what I needed." The Chair-man sounded very confused.

"Yes, but no harm in looking at what he has to offer. I had asked him to synthesize and analyze a set of documents on warfare. I am sure he has a terrible presentation. But the amount of work that would have gone in to analyze the huge document should not go waste. Why trouble the Star-boy? Let him start on a platform, and he will take off brilliantly." The Web-man said convincingly.

The Chair-man looked worried after he hung up. He thought the whole process was supposed to be as easy as getting the right person; the star-boy seemed like the right person. Why would the Star-boy need the presentation from Yuvan? Can't he develop his own? Is the Star-boy actually capable?

The Web-man, on the other hand, was worried. "They will all mess it up. I will have to do this myself. I will get the document from Yuvan, feed it to the star-boy and then we will win over the councilors. We don't need that stupid Chair-man after that. We will soon win the trust of the king, and then we will conquer the whole world."

This time the Thought Dimension was very different. It was different from Etash's Thought Dimension. It was different from Inu's Thought Dimension.

"We can move into a generic Thought Dimension like this one, with proper focus of course. This is a general medium to explore the multiverse," explained Inu.

Several billion bright cells were revolving around. The cells formed several networks resembling the neural network.

He was totally speechless. He quickly understood what the cells stood for.

"This is like watching a swarm of ants. The thoughts of so many people. The related cells moving across many oceans, jumping around. How to make out anything in this mess?"

"We have several ways to find the right thought when needed. With a lot of focus and meditation, the sages of the past could read the swarm and find the data they needed. These days we have the big data analytics on the cloud – the Muzoop. Come let me show you the infrastructure."

Wooosh, they seemed to be on the clouds, and the clouds had numbers!!

".....and the cloud 9 symbolizes happy sentiment?"

"Hey, we just wanted to have some fun. The clouds just symbolize categories of the neural networks. What we have here is several cells from several souls all working together to synthesize each other's data. The cells that are related synchronize with each other easily. Over a huge network, every cell is related to the other."

"But, don't the cells die?"

"The body cells die, yes. However, the cells that are part of the soul, the ones that are in the *Kundalini*, they have an infinite life. They are not bound by space or time. What is working here is samples of such cells obtained from several souls."

"...And you have created a big cluster of the cells to combine the processing power, the ideas and the memories of billions of souls."

"Yes.."

"Ok, can we go to any point of time and watch what is happening?"

"Kind of, basically there is no time for this. It is more like individual incidents have all been stored and referenced through the label, row key mechanism. The label can be thought of as time. So we can even have events from the future here because of the nature of this storage."

"Can we look into future and find how this will all end?"

"No, I don't understand this completely. So I cannot explain why not. However, The Professor tells us not to even think of it. He has forbidden us from opening any data related to the future. Some kind of law of nature, I guess."

Etash seemed thoughtful at this. "I'm not sure I like The Professor anymore. He is hiding a lot from me. He is projecting me to be the savior but doesn't tell me anything. Can he hear what we speak now?!!"

"Maybe. Right now we are in the general thought dimension. Here, people in the vicinity can hear us. It is like chatting over a public network. A person with an intent to read your conversation will find a way to do it. If we discuss inside each other's thought dimension, then it is different. That's more like chatting over a highly encrypted network, and one can join by invitation only.

"Hmm, but there were several people in your thought. Including that buffalo."

"The people in my thought were all invited by me."

"Did you invite the buffalo too?!"

"He is powerful. He can do anything and can go anywhere. Except that he is not the thinking kind and would never dream of insubordination. So he mostly goes were The Professor asks him to go."

"Hmm." He started to think that he needed to get The Buffalo on his side. The Professor seemed vague about a lot of things.

"Can we find out a pattern of these attacks by the *Patali* and the various weapons used in these wars?"

"Yes, let us get into a comfortable room" She started descending to the bottom-most cloud, cloud 1.

She led them into a room. The room had a board that read "Reserved for meetings from time to time."

"We are beyond space and time right now. Reserving against time is difficult. So the reservation is for whenever people are in it." She said and giggled realizing the irony.

They sat at a desk with a desktop on it. Inu logged into it and opened a report. With some proficient keystrokes, she brought up a report on the number of attacks "We have several from future as well. But most of the future data is ciphered as you can see. Looks like an additional level of encryption. Here, see this. The attacks are mostly organized on the human head. They seem to somehow take over key people of the era and try to push their agenda through them" Inu said pointing to the screen.

He started analyzing "The *Patali* folks attack through the leaders of humans. The screen shown by professor earlier had this darkening of multiple universes. That attribute there, what does it represent?"

"That's so one can recognize a *Patali* soul and a human soul."

"Have all the past attacks been by the *Patali* souls?"

"No. Of course, many of the wars have been due to *Patali*. It is just about who feels powerful at a given time. Powerful enough to challenge humanity. Then there is imbalance and wars happen. ."

"I think we know for now is sufficient. Let us return to the island. The Buffalo may get suspicious."

Chapter 30

"This seems like the right font. This will impress the Chair-man." Isha said confidently.
Yuvan focused on his computer screen. He hadn't used computers that much and wasn't comfortable with PowerPoint presentations.

Isha stood and looked at the screen. She frowned. She then went to a corner of the room and looked at the screen. Something was not right. She then stood upside down on her head. Oh yes, it seemed perfect now.

"You need to move the header on top of the slides. It feels weird to have content first and then the header."
Both started working on the plan discussed. They had to do something to set things right and find a role for themselves. Being manipulated and played on was demeaning.
It had started getting dark outside.

"Shall we have dinner and then work?" Yuvan had this weird habit. He had to eat on time.

"Goinnnnnnnnnnnnnnn…Goinnnnnnnnnnnnnnnnnnnnnn" the sound was reverberating. It was echoing…it was going into one's very being!

Inu, Etash, and The Buffalo were heading in a valley through a large canyon with huge red clay walls on both sides.

The Buffalo had an air of someone with extreme knowledge and was heading the party.

"Oh wow!" Inu gasped.

Etash almost gasped too.

Ahead of them, an ancient man was upside down hanging in the air and meditating.

The sound was vivid now "Goinnnnnnnnnnnn…………Goinnnnnnnnnnnnnnnnn n"

"He looks like the picture in that book," Etash whispered.

"Yes, it seems to be him," said Inu.

The Buffalo bowed with a lot of respect and sat down. Yes! Actually sat in dhyana mudra.

Etash and Inu also followed suit.

"Maybe he will speak from his position, or maybe he will come closer to us?" thought Etash.

"Hey folks, Om Namo Narayanaya! I was expecting you." , the voice came from behind.

A very transparent man, seemingly in rags was standing behind them. One could just make an outline of the man's features.

"Gruuuunnnnnnnnnnttttttttt, Sir, all due respect." said The Buffalo without turning back, his tail swatted a fly off lazily though.

Now there seemed to be a breeze around them. The transparent man's clothes did not move a bit even though the breeze seemed quite strong. The breeze seemed to be coming from him, not just from around. It was like sitting in front of a fan. The transparent man slowly came closer and sat in front of them.

"Auuuuuuuuuuuuuuuuuummmmmmmmmmmmm mm!" the transparent man seemed to be dramatizing, very similar to how The Professor delivered his lectures.

"Gruuuunnnnnnnnntttttttt …Sir, we thought it is time."

"You think it is time, already!!? Oh dear!" the old man seemed a tad bit uncomfortable. He slowly shifted his legs even while remaining in the asana." My legs hurt sitting in the same posture for long."

"Sir, shall we tell him the truth then?"

"Truth?! Oh yes, right!", 'the man' said absently.

"Here's the truth! This man is Wind-man. He is your father. Now I have to leave. Will meet you in the ashram near the beach." The Buffalo just disappeared.

Etash stood there, with his mouth slightly opened, and a frown on his face, still trying to fathom what The Buffalo just said.

The Wind-man now got up and walked towards Etash.

"I am your father, and this is my island."

"If you say so!! You are centuries old. How?!"

"Great…has this boy been like this always? Asking the most stupid question at the right time?", the Wind-man asked Inu. "Son, Relax! It will all come back to you." The Wind-man now held a hand above Etash's head and slowly massaged his neck and crown of the head as if pulling something up.

Etash slowly closed his eyes and went into a trance.

"Ok, Etash will now remember everything. But for your benefit, let me explain a few things. There are ways in which one can have children. One can do it the way normal humans do, of course, pretty elegant I would say. There are other ways.", the dramatic pause followed.

Inu knew better than to interrupt.

"I was a little bored and wanted to do some thought experiment. I thought of a beautiful soul who would be very strong, one who is very intelligent, Whose power of thought could be useful to all those who seek him. I did alright I guess. He has some great ideas or so it seems. He is, after all, born from 'thought.' He attracts a lot of negative souls though. *Patali* are constantly looking for him. It seemed safe to make him forget his strength so that he could be peaceful. And now it's time. Something is happening maybe, and his intelligence would help. Getting you here seems to be the handiwork of The Professor, the old guile man that he is.", the wind-man finally finished.

"We do have a major attack. *Patali* people seem to be taking over the multiverse one mind at a time. Maybe The Professor wanted you to guide your son." said Inu.

"I know him well. He is trying some experiment on me for sure. Anyways, let us think about it later. There is an attack, is it?!! Can't The Professor handle it? Is it that big?"

"Yes, on the measuring scale the count came at 9.2," said Inu.

The Wind-man took a deep breath. "Hmm, grave it is! Have you got an army ready?. Why would *Patali* waste so much energy? Usually, it is a 6.2 type attack, and then everything balances out. Everyone is happy. Why 9.2?!! What's our plan of defense?"

"We have a group in the ghost township. The Professor says the plan is to be able to have our soul cells split up across the universe and to take up positions around and get a larger view when the attack happens. I was supposed to find this message on 'art of war with *Patali*' or something like that. I found it with a person called Joisa. He, however, said that only Etash can decipher the message. I haven't been able to discuss with him though."

"Hmm, and you are?"

"I am a new one. I'm a gifted soul too. I'm born out of the need for time in the current world. The very need for a time created me out of the excess amount of time during rains. So you can say I'm the daughter of time and rain. Then The Professor found me. The group I hear finds all the gifted souls. I have been part of the group building the cloud, so I am aware of all the stuff. However, I do not know you."

"Hmm, I'm much older for people to remember. The Professor, The Buffalo and me, we go back several centuries. In fact, we stopped the cycle of birth and death for ourselves several centuries ago. "

A pause, this time the Wind-man seemed to be lost in thought.

"The attacks were all about taking over the main character of a story and then making the character write the rest of the story. It never worked though. The story deviated, went off-course and finally it had to flow towards its destiny. It always did. We were just some agents to help the story, that's all! Ravana,

Duryodhana, Hitler .. they just got taken over. The end was all the same. Destiny=Story. That's what we found. Stories had their own flow, and nothing could change the flow."

"I don't understand. Why do people try winning over the good? The rule clearly says there cannot be an imbalance."

"Who would define good? It is subjective. Everyone can think of themselves as good in their own boundaries. It is complicated. I have never questioned myself on this so much. Ok, let us head to the ashram. Etash will remember everything now."

Chapter 31

"Sir, I'm a poor chariot driver. I need to take care of my children. How much can I reduce."
The Web-man had his aura. He had his style. He would not say a number out loud. He would not name a price verbally. It was below his dignity.
He wrote a number on a piece of paper and handed it over to the chariot driver.
"Sir!!"
"Ok, no go?" The Web-man wrote another number and handed it over to the chariot driver.
"Sir!!"
The Web-man was done with all the papers he had. He wrote on his palm and showed it.
"sir"
This went on for a while. Finally, when The Web-man started removing his trouser to write on his boxers, the chariot driver gave up. "How can I explain to this stupid man that I cannot read?" He gave up shrugged and got his chariot ready. He had a vague idea of the direction of the kingdom. He had to give it a try. Anything was better than watching this crazy man undress and write everywhere.

"I am what I am. I am made of the atoms and molecules. What was once you, is me. My cells, my soul's cells have some references for every you. So we are all one." Etash suddenly woke up, startled. Was that his thought?

He was lying down on an oily table. Somebody seemed to have dripped him in oil. Inu was there, in a corner, sleeping in her chair and there was that

Wind-man who was introduced as his father. He was smiling, constantly and was upside down, in the asana.

"Yes, that was your thought and profound thought that was." The Wind-man spoke, "Relax a bit. You needed some regular oil massage to keep your body cool, as you remembered everything."

"I am a bait, isn't it? The Professor is putting me up as bait. I can feel it. I see it clearly."

"Hmm, you have been thinking about the purpose for you being called into the war. Individuals are just small pebbles in the great flow of the story. Didn't The Professor speak to you about the great story and how we need to just get going according to the flow?"

"It just worries me. This whole thing! It is not wrong. But something is missing in it."

"Don't do that! This is just the sudden dawn of clarity speaking, I understand. But control the surge of power. We need to deduce things slowly. We have time for it."

Inu slowly stood up.

"It will do you good to take Inu out for a few days. It will prepare you for the war. You may get a clear idea as well. It will help, believe me. I suggest we all go on a trip to the earth. We have to meet The Professor anyways."

"Understood," said Etash and Inu together.

"I suggest we go to this place called Qooty, on our way to the ghost town. I hear it is interesting. It will help you both think things over."

Inu was angry at hearing that "So again it is the same, is it? I'm just someone who helps the hero calm down, provides support. Why can't this be about me? Maybe, Etash is supposed to help me realize the way to split my soul into the multitude, and then I go blasting through *Patali* army."

"It is possible. I would not deny that. Remember, it is always the story that is important. We are just part of it."

This reminded Etash of the lecture of The Professor. "Story is important. Ramayana, Mahabharata, the Story of Ashoka had a life."

Chapter 32

"Is this location safe enough" Isha was keen to start discussing

"yeah, we seem to be far off. The Chair-man seems to be completely off track, so I don't think anybody would be following us" Yuvan said

They had walked into the center of the kingdom. Right now they were in a market place. They chose a coffee shop to sit and discuss.

"The actual ideas of war are safe in your book. Let us put it into another presentation. We would need it for the king" Isha said eagerly.

"Do you really think the king will give us an audience?"

"Surely the king would be smart enough to understand that the web solution is a concoction of somebody's imagination. Kings have to be smart. They can get killed for being dumb. I'm sure there will be hundreds of people waiting to take his place."

The Professor was sitting at his desk deep in thought.

"The Wind-man should have been here by now. He has the power to destroy the *Patali* using his strong storm waves. Concentrating all the *Patali* towards one point would be the key. That would help us fight the battle from a position of strength rather than spreading thin. I had to put up the kid as bait. There was no option. Intelligent he is, but he is not required for this battle. It is us: the troika since time immemorial."

He looked apologetic. "Getting Etash into the mess was not right. But he has it in him to attract the negative energy."

He now stood up and went towards *Eshwara's* photo on the wall "Oh *Eshwara*, save us. I hope my plan is in line with the story."

The *Patali* were watching him. They were very emotional seeing the human Professor praying. They sniffed, it was almost as if they had a nose. The *Patali* professor walked in. "I hope you guys……" He stood still, watching his team members crying. "What the….." He immediately called the head chef, "Increase the green chilly in their diet. We can't have such softies in our army."

Chapter 33

"Stop, stop right there."

The Chariot stopped. The Web-man, who had been sitting at the back, completely drunk, fell off from the chariot and rolled over into a valley. He further rolled on into a river flowing through the valley.

A short man jumped into the river after him. After a few minutes, he came out carrying The Web-man.

The chariot driver helped the short man, and both of them reached back to the top. They placed The Web-man on a flat surface by the chariot. After trying out pumping the chest and then mouth to mouth resuscitation they were almost ready to give up when he suddenly coughed. He was back.

The short man heaved a sigh of relief.

"Sir, he saved you," the chariot driver told The Web-man pointing towards the short man.

"Oh, my savior! Come here" The Web-man hugged the short man and started crying "you name your price. I want to compensate."

The short man hesitated. He did not know the numbers. "How about say 1/3rd of what you have?"

The Web-man immediately stood up and kicked the short man where it hurt. "Let us go," he said to the chariot driver.

"Listen, how about we make ourselves useful and feel better about everything?" said Inu.

"How?" , asked Etash puzzled.

Inu: "You are an expert in Philosophy and Physics. I have seen you reading *Kundalini* Shakti, Quantum Mechanics, Matter Transmission, Quantum Travel."

Etash: "So?!"

Inu: "Try and bring it all together."

A bell rang at a nearby church. Etash went into deep thought. "The theory is, a story has a life. In that case, can a subplot be introduced into a story to change its life?" , Etash face brightened as if he had come up with a path-breaking theory like in the scientific world.

"When you first saw me what was our opinion of me?" he asked Inu.

"A very studious person, a man interested in books. You hardly seemed to care about anything else."

"Right, the story of a nerd. Let us try to see if my first impression on people changes for other people if I change my characters look." He held her hand and took her to the commercial street- a busy street with a lot of small local retail shops. You think of it, and you will get it here.

After a brief search, he found what he was looking for. He asked her to wait outside and stepped in.

She started rolling with laughter when he stepped out.

"How do I look?" , asked Etash excited.

"A total wannabe. Like you are trying too hard, not sure for what though!", she said amidst giggles.

"See! We have potentially changed the narrative about me in the story. I have read a blog of some software engineer that gives me an idea. He joined a project with a good name. But as he moved forward and tried to live up to his reputation, some evil elements in the team who had their own agenda, started spreading stories about him not in line with what was actually going on. He was portrayed as an excellent orator, but someone who could not work hands-on with the code. That he was a speaker and not a 'do-er, they said. Not much later, they succeeded in making that storyline real. Involved parties started contradicting him in his ideas from different directions. He lost focus, failed in his work. He was humiliated and moved out of the project. He worked hard on his coding and learned new skills.

The evil elements, different ones this time though with a different agenda, started spreading a story that he can only code, he cannot speak effectively to clients and managers. They succeeded once again. The software engineer lost his mental balance, went for therapy and finally retired. He is now some remote corner, away from the industry, successfully doing his own thing."

"What are you hinting at?" Inu was not able to get the drift.

"By adding a new narrative to a story - we can call it a 'rumor', - the main story's plot changes. My project for the year was to see how a subplot can be introduced to the main story and how it can alter the flow of the story. Can destinies be made."

"I think I understand what you are getting at. Its somewhat but not exactly like, when you want to give bad news, so you talk about something worse.

And then when the receiver is devastated, you tell them that was not true and then give the real bad news. It is better received, believe it or not. Another incident I heard, is where a big corporation that wanted to stop paying the bonus to its employees started a rumor that the company is doing so bad that employees may not get their salaries. Finally, when employees found that it was just the bonus that was being stopped, the employees were happy."

"Exactly, but here, we need something deeper, something that can alter the plot."

 Inu was all excited.

Chapter 34

"My good man. Let us stop here for the night." The Web-man told the chariot driver enthusiastically.
"But, sir, it is just past midday. We just had our lunch!"
"You need to learn to loosen up man! Take a break. I will teach you how to be happy. Now go and enquire at that Inn, if they have rooms."
"Yes sir" the chariot driver was excited. He had never been called a good man. To be told that he would be invited to have fun, he was almost on cloud nine.

"And don't worry about money. Pay the inn-owner whatever it takes."

The inn was a little to the shady side. People of all types were already filling into their pub in the cellar. Loud music was playing.

"This is what I call music man." The Web-man said rocking his head.

They were looking from the darkness. They were the PSI. They liked calling themselves 'Intelligentia.' In fact, they were very happy if people introduced this fact several times over. They virtually ruled the *Patali*. They made sure they had clout over the entire administrative apparatus of *Patali* including their king and ministers. Organizing regular wars helped in keeping themselves relevant. After a few wars, they had realized that conventional warfare would drain them out. They needed to be able to keep going. The only way for that would be to corrupt the enemy souls. They could dispense any number of enemy souls without alarming their own people.

A lot of humans had heard of PSI. They just dismissed it as an urban myth. Why would someone spend all their energy in developing and nurturing hatred? Humans going bad was probably just a phenomena, like tomatoes rot. This thought process of progressive humans worked well for the PSI. They worked in the background to build a large empire for themselves. They got a lot of funds from the *Patali* kingdom as well as from many entities that hated humans. Yes, several entities hated humans, Vrushalas for example. PSI had made *Patali* the center for all human haters.

As they looked at the progress of the *Patali* Professor, they seemed happy.

"The Professor is doing a good job. He has corrupted a lakh of souls in each of the universes. Impressive." A voice made an observation.

"Let us present this at out 'General Human Hater Club.' We need approval for our next set of the budget." Another voice concluded.

Chapter 35

"You know, these drinks, are never pure. I'm not able to feel a thing. I can manage to drink a barrel of these. Hey, look at that, pretty girls dancing on the stage. Ye hooo, ho, hoo. Come on let us get on stage."

The chariot driver sat there, clearly confused. There didn't seem to be any stage in the pub. There didn't seem to be any girls in the pub either. There were a few men arm wrestling and a few men surrounding them betting on who would win.

"Hey, hey. Look at my dance" The Web-man was balancing himself on his one hand and hopping. It was amazing as he had had a barrel already.

The chariot driver noticed a few dangerous looking men laughing and pointing towards The Web-man. His sixth sense alerted him. He knew the pubs of the land and how nasty it can get. He quickly went to The Web-man and tried to calm him down.

"Look, look my dear man. Look into my eyes. Do you understand what I say? These are ears, Y-E-A-R-S", he spelled it out. "Got it? Now LISTEN carefully. This is a fun place. If you can't have fun, please go back to the room. Do not disturb me" The Web-man was beyond reason.

The Wind-man met Etash and Inu at the Qooty town bridge. "We must leave for the ghost town now. The Professor must be worried."

Inu and Etash just looked at each other.

Etash spoke "Listen, Pitaji. We came up with some analysis. We read the scripture provided By Mr. Joisa. It is pointing to stone encryption in deep forest on outskirts of the ghost town. It says the stone encryption has secrets for winning wars against the *Patali*."

The Wind-man hushed them up and whispered: "let us discuss this with The Professor. Too many ears here. Get ready. We take the next available bus to the ghost town." The Wind-man said and walked towards their hotel to get his luggage.

As the Wind-man was out of earshot, Inu whispered "Do you think the plan worked? Would we be able to divert the focus from you?"

"I would think so," Etash said though he didn't sound confident. "Once they are all diverted we will work on some plan. It should all be fine. Don't worry." He seemed to be reassuring himself.

They had spent the past couple of days going around the beautiful town of Qooty while they formulated their plan. They had decided that they had enough of being the bait. Now it was their time to rule the rooster. From now they would control this war.

"Something about a scripture. Yes, somewhere deep in the forest." A *Patali* was speaking on his mobile phone. He obviously seemed to be giving status to his master. He had done a good job of following Etash and Inu closely. There were some not so important things they discussed like going to the cloud and manipulating the war. The *Patali* did not want to call his boss with all the stupid details. He knew he was experienced enough to know what information would be interesting to his boss. The look on his face told, his boss was happy with him as well. He would probably get some extra load of virgin olive oil once back in *Patal*. *Patali* were crazy for virgin olive oil.

Chapter 36

"I'm feeling helpless. I have this presentation from that stupid Yuvan. I can't make much of it. I don't understand where to get a net as big as the kingdom? I can't even reach The Web-man." The Chair-man was huddled in his cabin with the star-boy. The Chair-man's superior sat at a distance and watched.

"Do you think that Yuvan is misleading us? It clearly seems to be a stupid idea." The Chair-man's superior came up with a smart question for a change.
The Star-boy clearly disagreed "No, Yuvan is incapable of anything. He hasn't even written a single line of a poem to date."

The Chair-man's superior gave up at this "You guys are competent enough to decide. Do let me know the budget you need."

The Chair-man was intrigued "So you say he has just come up with a brilliant idea but is incompetent or is it a brilliantly incompetent idea?"

"I'm just saying that it is not new. Yuvan just compiled ideas from the books given by our great Web-man. However, the idea has been presented badly. The fonts are all bad, the color is bad, and also no thought has been given to framework. One should develop their own framework for such things. My lead The Web-man has thought me some secrets on how to develop

"Hey, my man." The professor came running like a young boy.

"Hey! You haven't grown old a bit" The Wind-man ran ahead like a kid too.

They embraced each other like two long lost friends. Only, they were two long lost friends.

"So it was all your idea, ahem. Why did you trouble Etash for it?" The Wind-man was mocking anger. He clearly seemed to enjoy all the attention.

"Come, let us sit comfortably and discuss. *Patali* are again up to it. We need you." The Professor led them into the hospital chamber. Etash, Inu and Wind-man had just arrived in the ghost town. Next few hours went in the two friends remembering their previous wars. They were speaking loudly and draining out mugs of drink.

"Sir," Etash was standing at a distance watching the old friends make merry. "Sir," this time he heard it and turned around. It was a member of Professor's army. He was kneeling in front of him with hands in front of the chest. "We have heard a lot about you. It is a privilege to see you. When do you plan to lead us into the war?" Etash stood speechless. The man had tears in his eyes. Clearly, he had seen hell and hated the *Patali*. He struggled to find the right answer. "Don't worry. Etash here has come up with some great plans. Victory will be ours. Now, do give us some privacy." It was the Professor. He had sneaked up them on seeing the army member near Etash. He held Etash by hand and took him to where Wind-man was seated. Inu and the Buffalo joined them. Finally, they all settled down to discuss the next course of action. Etash brought up the topic of Joisa's message.

"The encrypted message suggests the path to the actual 'art of defeating *Patali*.'" Etash said "The actual message is under a stone in this very town. It is encrypted. This message can be decrypted by one old man who also stays in this town. We made some inquiry on the way. This old man is from Andaman. He has been in the town for a long time."

"This stone encryption seems to be very important. We did do a lot of work on ciphers and languages. Remember that time in Germany?" Said The Professor.

The Wind-man just smiled.

"Let The Buffalo take a few people to find the cipher guy. Let us find the stone. Etash and Inu, you stay here."

A look into a map of the area on the latest mapping software revealed a few possible points where the stone engraving may be found.

"The area behind that haunted shopping complex. That seems interesting" Said The Wind-man.

"What's interesting? It is not showing any large stone!!"

"No, but any haunted place will have interesting things nearby. We may find a lost soul too. I think we should start from there."

"Ok, you are again at it. I can see the mischief in your eye. Let us head towards the complex then."

Soon everything was decided. The Buffalo to find the Andaman man, Professor and Wind-man to find the stone scripture.

The Professor gave a strong speech to his army before his departure. "Etash has revealed the plans to me. We get the secret scripture, and then the war begins. As soon as I have the scripture, I will send a message to you on the location of the war. Please wait for my signal. Etash and Inu will be here with you. They will be focusing on several aspects, so please do not disturb them. Let them strategize in peace and provide us the light of their wisdom."

Inu turned towards Etash. He turned towards her as well. They heard it "Etash's name is an inspiration. However, he is to remain at the back as inspiration only!"

Chapter 37

"Aah, sir you are awake" the chariot driver's voice is bland. The Web-man looks for a hint of sarcasm but doesn't find any.
"It was a tough fight there. You are a scared man. You should have seen the way I handled those goons."

The chariot driver looked at the black eye of The Web-man. He was barely able to open it.

"Yes, sir. I heard."
"These things are common, man! You should have seen the fight of the millennia I had got into a few years back. I don't get into this these days. I prefer not showing my strength."
"Yes, sir. I understand"
"Do we leave now?"
"I think so, sir. I have packed our stuff into the chariot. Have packed some food for on the way. We are set."

The Web-man tried to get up from his bed and groaned. The inn manager had been kind enough to get a doctor and plaster The Web-man up.
 The chariot driver put all his effort to lift The Web-man off the bed and carry him to the chariot.

The Professor and the Wind-man with his stick started towards the complex. They were trying to find the stone scripture as per the plan. The road from the hospital took a turn towards a large theatre and then further headed along a basketball court. Here towards the left, there was a pathway leading into a forest. The Professor and the Wind-man walked past the snakes, they seemed to rush away in fear, as if they had seen an eagle.

"This is too steep for my age" grunted The Wind-man."Sometimes these stone carvings are just some pretext to hide interesting information, the interesting information is usually below the stone." he said.

Etash and Inu sat at the hospital with a bemused look on their face.

"How come they got a probable location? Is the stone actually there?! I thought we had just spread a rumor. Wouldn't the man from Andaman story get over quickly? The Buffalo would soon find we were lying. " Etash asked.

"The Andaman man angle is covered. I did some research before providing you that data. There is actually a family living at the outskirts of the ghost town. However, what confuses me is the stone. That was totally from our imagination. How did that appear in the probable location? The main story seems to continue to find a way of its own! I hope our next steps work." Inu replied.

Meanwhile, The Buffalo was leading his team on the 'Mission Andaman Man.'

"Gruuuunnnnnnnnnnnnttttttt ...what are we looking for? An old man and a wife, from Andaman?" The Buffalo had taken the form of a wrestler. They all went to the nearest bus stand. "We can get all information from the Paan Shop near a bus stand, and the best way is to......."

Hanging from a tree branch didn't feel safe. The paan shop guy was shivering. He probably had never done this asana , or yoga for that matter.

"What is it you want? T....t...ttt.......t....take all the p..p..p..paan." he blurted.

"Ok, paan is great. Maybe, but not the folded one that you feed other animals. I prefer a normal leaf. Anyways, do you know of a man living here somewhere, who is married to a girl from Andaman and is probably old?"

"What...?!!! And you..yyy..you did this to me to get information?" the man was shocked. His stuttering disappeared "This person was living in the forest at the edge of the town, on the other side. He used to rear cows and buffaloes. He delivered milk to the houses on the other edge. Look for the boards that read sector 2."

The wrestler shaped Buffalo tried a few paan from the box. "Ummm, not bad. But nothing can beat fresh green grass. Gruuuunnnnnnnnnntttttt"

Chapter 38

"Narayana, Narayana" The sage was walking on the middle of the road. They had just gotten into a path through the forest. The Chariot driver was a little nervous and did not want to stop there. The motion of the chariot made the Web-man doze off.

"You have been manipulated. He was after all a subordinate.
Narayana!Narayana!"

The Web-man suddenly woke up. He was very clear on insubordination; He cannot let it happen!
"What?!! Where?! Who?!"
"You aren't as intelligent as you think you are. Narayana! Narayana!"
"Silent sage! You are speaking too much. "
"Your anger is misdirected!. Show it where it needs to be shown! Someone is manipulating your system with impunity. He has betrayed your trust. He has a document with secrets of war, and he hasn't given it to your star-boy. He wants to become famous himself."
"I will not let it happen. I will get that man arrested." The Web-man got up in a hurry and lost balance. He fell forward onto his bed and dozed off.

There was a meeting going on at Patal. Tho Professor of Patal and his team were huddled together in a conference room.

The Professor of the *Patali* said "I think it is high time I get into the thick of things. The PSI need status and sitting here, I can't say much. Let us enter the town." He was restless. All their plans had hinged on kidnapping Etash. Etash had however seemed to do nothing in the past few days. They had, of course, lost track of him briefly. Now with every key human warrior in the town, it seemed better to get into it as well. It was easier to analyze the situation from up close.

"But *Patali* can't penetrate the protective covering. We cannot go in." said a team member.

"Yes. But we can take over the minds of a few vulnerable humans. In their mind, we can lead them. The protection can't stop humans and cannot detect us in their mind." said The Professor of the *Patali*.

The plan was ready. The team members started looking for vulnerable humans at the edge of the forest.

Meanwhile, The Professor of *Patali* went into another room. A few of his team members followed him. This was the next level meeting. The nameplate on the door of the room said "Level 2 Meeting Room". "My dear leads" The Professor of *Patali* addressed team members who had followed him. The team members were clearly leaders for something. The Professor continued "I have handpicked each one of you. I know what you are capable of. You have been working with me on the plan. It is execution time. Just keep an eye for The Professor of humans and The Wind-man. They will emerge into the open space soon. I will lead them into the open space. Capture them and send them into their own distant memory as per the plan. Is that understood? "

"Yes, sir" The leads seemed in very high spirits. After all, they had just got a new title. They had just been conferred with the title "Lead."

"Great. All the best then. I'm hoping to have a great status report for the PSI."

Patalis, All set for the war.

Chapter 39

Yuvan and Isha, are they made for each other?

Yuvan and Isha were unaware. They are enjoying their new-found liking for each other.

Some hooded figures stood huddled in the corner of the room.

"Why are we observing them?" the one on the left asked.

"What are we observing for?" the one on the right had a bigger question.

"Just keep observing. I'm sure we will know, soon." The center intelligent-sounding one said. He was a candidate for PSI. He had already added a surname to his name tag: 'Intelligent.'

Yuvan was trying to show off his skills to Isha. He was trying to balance a coin on his forehead. Surprisingly, Isha seemed to be interested. She looked like a girl in love.

Meanwhile a very interesting conversation was on nearby.

"Isn't this an orphan universe? We like orphan universes don't we? Once the universe is cut-off, we are done with it isn't it?" the one on the left was clearly not done asking questions.

"There is more to it. Look at the way they are practicing. They must be getting ready for the war. He must be some hidden warrior with great skills. Our corrupted soul would be coming here soon. He is being led here. Until then, we observe" The intelligent one replied. The *Patalis* were in the orphan universe!

Inu and Etash had decided to enter the Thought Dimension to further execute their plans. They were now in the cloud infrastructure. They had hatched the plan to mislead everyone. Accordingly, The Professor and The Wind-man were hunting for this non-existent stone. The Buffalo and its team were on the lookout for an innocent old man who knew nothing. By the time people would realize, they had to execute their next part of the plan.

"We have changed everyone's focus. Earlier you were the attraction. Right now people are moving in different directions. To that extent, our plan has succeeded. I'm a little uneasy about the stone angle though. The Professor would soon find out there is no stone. Anyways, what next?" asked Inu.

"Let us feed a thought into all the infected people of the multiverse. A thought that would make them all move towards one direction. It would be easy to manage them all in one place."

"Thought?! Like what? When we were discussing the plan earlier, I remember you said about moving everyone in a single direction. You referred to some story of The Great Bangle. Is it the same as that stupid movie which has had three sequels already? I have had to watch it all thanks to my boyfriends!" Inu said.

"Yes, I got the idea based on the movie and its original novel. People in it are all competing for The Great Bangle, and the one who wins it is called The Lord of The Bangle. We should make our infected people believe the same. We can say the Bangle is located below a stone. A stone which is present in an old haunted town. The coordinates should match our town. The Professor and The Wind-man are there. The war would be easier. " There was a conviction in Etash's voice.

"Lord of the Bangle?!! That would work. That would also mean there will be a war! Can't we avoid bloodshed?" Inu seemed to agree. But she would have preferred to avert the war entirely.

"I don't want war either. However, I'm not sure it can be entirely averted. The infected souls have to be corrected. When there is a war, The Professor will slice the infections out of them. This would reduce the strength of *Patali* who have infected them. With that, I hope they would surrender. From time to time bloodshed is necessary to restore the balance of the multiverse." Etash's said.

"In a way, we are taking revenge on The Professor. He was putting both of us off. Now we are the ones that would be making matters easy for them! What an anti-climax for The Professor's plans!" Inu sniggered and turned back. To an onlooker, her smile would have seemed maniacal.

Everybody needs a purpose in life. Everyone needs a chapter of their own in the great story, at least a section, to be clear.

Etash was feeling excited too. "We would be needed during the war as well. Let us see how this goes." He said confidently.

Chapter 40

The Web-man was restless. "I need to call The Chair-man." He pulled out his mobile and dialed the number.

"Listen. Psst, psst, psst" The Web-man spoke.

"I get it. I will get him arrested. But," The Chair-man seemed confused on the other side.

"It is imperative that we get the original war plan from him. Arrest him and then psst, psst."

"Yes, but, we have already prepared a better presentation. We plan to 'webify' the kingdom. The Star-boy is already on it."

"Hmm, that seems like a good idea. What was that sage talking about then?! Nevertheless, we can't be too careful. Arrest him and then psst, psst."

"Hmm, got it, mate. Just one question. What is psst, psst?"

"!!" The Web-man banged his head onto the chariot."Just hang him upside down and pour oil on him while rotating him. It is standard procedure. How come you are a Chair-man?!"

The Professor of *Patali* along with his team surveyed the landscape around the town carefully. They needed some vulnerable humans.

"That Old man. And that old woman there. Wow, and all the children and grandchildren. They look like a good bet. Let us enter them." The Professor of *Patali* said to his team.

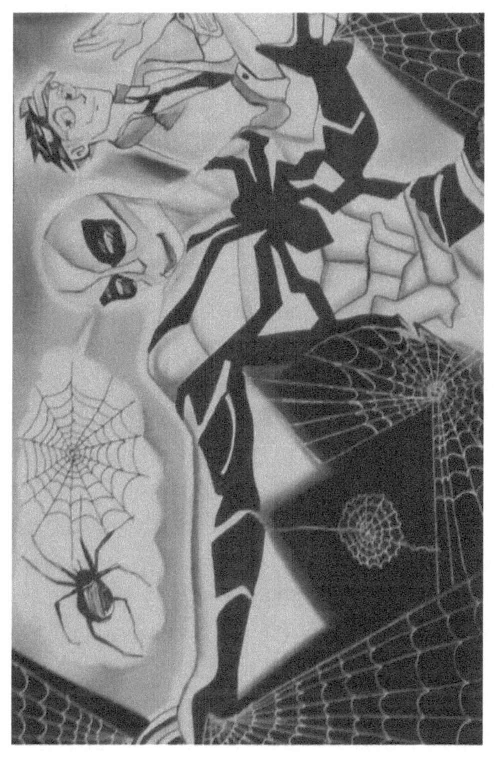

Web-man with his protégé, the Star-boy

The *Patali* all seemed to clap their hands in excitement. Them not having hands seemed just a small glitch in the excitement. They were merely dark souls. Several generations ago some brilliant one had devised a dress, and to this day the *Patali* wore a blanket, it gave them shape, it made them recognize each other as the one, the other, etc.

As fate may have it, The old man picked up by the *Patali* was the Andaman man. He and his family unaware of the horrific things that were to happen to them were deep in conversation. They had troubles of their own. He had migrated from Andaman and settled at the edge of the town, several decades ago. Everything had worked well for him. Great income from selling milk, great family, nice air, what more can a man ask for? However, disaster struck a year back in the form of a rumor. Somebody had spread a word that the town was soon going to be at the center of a horrible war. People in the town would be destroyed. What started out as a rumor, spread like wildfire. Soon, the townsfolks believed in it. People started leaving the town. Within a few months, the whole town was deserted. After the town had been deserted and turned into the present day ghost town, his income had drastically reduced. He had managed for a few months, with the thought that the town will be occupied again. It will have people bustling around once again. But now it looked like a closed chapter. He was distraught.

"How do we run this family. The last of the people staying in the town has left. It is just a ghost town now. Maybe we should go to one of the cities" the old man's voice seemed tired.

"Father, we have never been to a city. It may corrupt us, you said. Now, how do we sustain there?" one of the sons said.

"That was all a lie. I just wanted to keep you guys innocent. These are difficult times. I invoke my parental rights to say we go to the cities."

"Well, in that case, father, I would like to share a secret. We have visited the city several times!! We used to hide at the back of one of the trucks that came to deliver hay and grocery. It was fun" said the son.

The father looked a little shocked, but it was too late to start worrying about it.

"I have probably been tough on them. My children would have made a decent living by now if I had let them migrate to the cities."

Wooosh. As the old man was speaking, suddenly, he felt a cold breeze enter his ears. He now seemed like a man possessed "I need to go into the ghost town...wha...I need to go into the town."

Woosh "I have to visit the town." , the son got up. He seemed possessed as well. The father got up. The entire family got up. The ones that were already up, before the woosh, they had a soul awakening.

It looked like a scene out of a zombie movie. The entire family as one started walking towards the town.

"I want to go to town."

"I want to go to town."

They kept saying every few minutes.

The *Patali* had possessed the family. They had a good understanding of the art of possession of human minds. However, they hadn't grasped the idea of human brains very well. The bodies were going out of control, and the thoughts were going berserk. The only way to control seemed to make the bodies speak out loud to hide the underlying feelings.

Chapter 41

"We just wanted to give the presentation to the king. It is here in this pen drive. Please take it. Just leave us alone."

Yuvan was hanging upside down.

The Chair-man was following The Web-man's plan.

"It is not about war plan anymore. So just keep quiet."

"Sir, we do not care about anything anymore. We want to go off to some far off land. We will not bother anyone" Isha was dipped in a cauldron of oil.

The Chair-man just walked off. He had had enough of it. He had to present the web idea to the councilors.

"What is this stupid guy up to?" Isha asked Yuvan. "He hasn't even heated the oil. What kind of yucky torture is it?"

"Ask me. I'm hung upside down," Yuvan said in a sarcastic tone.

"Let me help you with that."

The Professor and The Wind-man had surprisingly managed to find a stone with scriptures on it. Etash's imaginary stone scripture was right in front of The Professor. This was probably another example of nature asserting its power.

"Should we dig up this stone?" The Wind-man was sitting with his back against the large black stone.

The Professor was sitting and trying to read the carvings on the other side of the stone "We need to pull out this stone, not that I agree with you on something being below...but we can't wait here. Let us take the stone with us back to the hospital and then if The Buffalo and the team haven't found the man we can try to help."

"ok great" The Wind-man was quickly on his feet. He plucked out the stone with his fingers...almost as if he were plucking a flower.

Woooshhhhhhhhhhhhh...

The wind started gushing out of the hole below the stone. There was something bright in there. The whole area turned floodlit.

"What is that?" The Professor tried to peer into the hole. Nothing was visible.

"We just have to walk-in. Nobody bothered with the stone these many years...it will be safe here for another few moments." , the Wind-man placed the stone inside an old cobbler's shop and put some leaves and branches on it. "There! It is safe now."

The Professor was looking blank. He looked at the hole and then at the cobbler's shop. The Wind-man walked in. He just walked into that unknown pit!!

The Professor knew The Wind-man well. This is how he handled things. If there was a switch which read "End of the world! Please do not touch.", he would be the first one to touch, open the switch and follow the wire till the mains.

The Professor jumped into the pit.

Woooosh wooosh... The stone flew out of the shop and landed on the hole covering it. There was no wind from the pit now, it was closed. Even the light...there was no trace of it.

Chapter 42

The Web-man hurried into the chairman's cabin. "Hurry up. Get the web idea going. Just have one big gap to the south of the kingdom." He said, without bothering to check who occupied the room.

That was his biggest mistake. There, bang in the middle of the cabin was a chair revolving. The entire cabin was empty.
The Web-man turned towards the door expecting someone to snigger. There was no one there.
He went to the Chair-man's desk. There was a diagram of the plan for web pasted there. "Hmm, this is a great plan. I can see your work Star-boy." thought The Web-man proudly.
"Hmm, they have probably gone to present it to the councilors. Let me go to the cellar and check that stupid Yuvan. He must be cooked well by now."

The cellar was easy to find. It was just next to the Chair-man's cabin. There was a big board "CELLAR" outside it.
The Web-man approached the door of the cellar. He knew something was wrong. His years of experience and his rich intelligence told him the birds had escaped the cage. Clear footmarks were going out of the cellar.

"Urrrgh, this Chair-man cannot even do work to completion. I will have to find these brutes myself." the Web-man hurried out tracing the footmarks.

On cloud 1, Etash and Inu were sitting at the computer panel. They were executing the plan. The plan that required them to cast the story of the bangle into the infected person's brain.

"This is a feature called multicast. We can enter the thoughts we want to broadcast. It will get broadcast to everyone we select, at once." said Inu.

"Awesome! So we just type in?" , Etash had not seen this before.

"This is much cooler than that. We can speak into the terminal. We have to use a cool, strong voice though. It should be persuasive."

"Ok do you think it should be me?" , Etash asked picking up the mic.

"No. I think this is my domain, my forte. Let me have a go at it." Inu grabbed the mic. She knew her calm, and soothing voice would do the trick.

"Alright then!" Etash urged her on.

"So what should I say? Maybe we should write this down." Inu was nervous.

"Sounds good!" Etash agreed. Inu knew this tone of Etash's. He would go into the garb of a person who understood nothing when he felt slighted. He probably wanted to speak into the terminal himself. He was like a kid who had seen a new toy.

She held his hand and made the expression of pleading. "What should we write?"

Etash could not do it anymore. That expression of Inu's, he could die for. "We say, "The life is all about The Bangle. Since time immemorial, the Bangle has been sought after. It has been with your forefathers. A band of thieves stole it. It is time to claim it back. Search for the Bangle. Everything else is not important anymore." And then say, 'A document describing where the Bangle is, describing a great penance to be undertaken to get it. This document is hidden in a forbidden, ghost township." And then just give coordinates of our town."

Etash paused for Inu to assimilate what he just said. He continued "And we would have everyone going to one place. Every infected person, at least. Everyone would head towards The Bangle. That would be easy for the troika – The Professor, The Wind-man and The Buffalo. They would cleanse the bad cells of these persons."

"Ok, here we go," Inu started speaking to the terminal.

Chapter 43

The councilors were all standing. They were clapping their hands. The Star-boy was in the middle of the floor. The Chair-man was beside him. They had given a presentation of a lifetime. The Star-boy's brain child, "Webification of kingdom" had just been presented to the councilors.

The lead of the councilors stepped ahead. She went onto the dais, held the mic and started to speak "People, as you all know, we have been trying to find out a plan to safeguard ourselves while we focus on usurping the neighboring kingdoms. It has been a long journey. Several people, several ideas later we seem to have got to a final workable idea." She looked at her fellow councilors and then continued, "I think today as a group I can say that we are happy to approve a budget of 50000."

The Chair-man could not believe his ears. He was expecting just a few. 50000 was just fantastic. Ofcourse, the billion he had asked for was just a number he had placed. The councillors never approved a budget more than a few hundred rupees at a time. They seemed phenomenally excited by his plan to approve Rs. 50000!
"Chair-man sir, as you step out, please collect the cheque for Rs.50,000/- from the finance manager."

The Chair-man's world was reeling. He had never heard of such a lot of money together.

"Sir, start your work on this web project of yours. Start by placing a web at the front door of the kingdom of Salsa. Let there be a dark red picture of our king at the center of the web. Next, you can do the same on king Katak. Soon everyone should start talking about the web. The web should serve as a warning. I'm sure we will have a few kings sending emissaries to us soon. Our king is frightening enough, the web and red color would just get them covering."

"Narayan Narayan... What are they up to? I must stop them," thought the wandering sage of the clouds. The wandering sage wandered around sharing information. He always had a significant role in every story of the universe.

Looking at Etash and Inu's, work, the wandering sage was worried. He knew at once that this would require some intervention.

"Let me go to the three pillars of the multiverse and ask them for help." The sage usually did this. He prodded people to act. He prodded people to act the way he wanted. Of course, the powers of the universe, the three pillars, knew everything and did not need prodding.

With immense meditation and strength, the sage soon invoked himself into the presence of the 3 great forces of the universe of universes. He looked around. It was a large palace somewhere without space or time.

"Narayan. Narayan! Oh, Lords!! Please stop them. They do not know what they are doing. We will have a big collapse."

The powers of the universe looked at each other and smiled.

"Oh, great sage! We understand your concern. You have been our great messenger from time immemorial. However, do not panic. The system never collapses. The multiverse is self-healing." They continued with a smile, "Nature has its own plans. The great story cannot be stopped. It will find its own path. The war was required to bring the multiverse in control. Inu and Etash will help in this. They will soon realize their role. The story will pick its characters."

"Narayan, Narayan. Your Maya is mesmerizing. I'm looking forward to the next events with interest." The Sage bowed with utmost reverence. He knew his role and his next steps.

Chapter 44

"What are these fools talking about?" The star-boy was agitated as they walked back to the chairman's cabin.

The chairman held the big cheque for 50000 in his hand. "Calm down man. This happens. Don't worry. We can manage great. I have a plan ready. We may just need a few soldiers. We have to attack from the left, then the right and then. "

"Stop right there" it was The Web-man. "You have messed it up sufficiently. That's enough"

"We just placed your idea in front of the councilors" The Chair-man retorted.

"Hmm, but so very badly that you have got this stupid fund. Give me that cheque."

The Web-man snatched the cheque, folded it, and kept it carefully in his pocket "Now, we have several things to be done. Send some guards to follow the oily footsteps towards the king's palace. Also, you, my star-boy, follow me. Let us discuss this over a drink."

The Web-man and the Star-boy went towards the house bar.

"Gruuuuunnnnnnnnnnntttttttt, how do we find this Old Man from Andaman? Let us ask that group walking towards us." The Buffalo and team were still searching for the Old Man who could decrypt. It was not a very difficult task for someone smart. There were hardly any humans in and near the town. Smartness was not The Buffalo's forte.

They had found a pathway at the north entrance of the town. It leads to the forest. It seemed obvious, even to The Buffalo, that there was some recent human activity. They slowly started combing the area.

After a while, they suddenly heard human voices. It sounded as if somebody was reciting some holy verses. The team moved towards the voices, stealthily. After a few steps, the pathway opened up into a large clearing. There was a stream flowing towards one side of the clearing. At a corner, there were several cows grazing. The warrior instinct in The Buffalo and the team made them alert. It would be evident to anybody who had watched enough action movies that there was an imminent attack. Somebody had left everything in a hurry. They would be hiding nearby.

The Buffalo and its team had formed a circle and were slowly turning. They were watching around for any sign of movement. The human voices were still coming from somewhere nearby. And then suddenly they appeared.

They were walking in a line. An old man in the front. An old woman behind him and then several people who looked like their family members. They were chanting, "I want to go to town. I want to go to town."

The simple townsfolks with complicated occupants noticed The Buffalo's team.

"We probably need to move closer to each other. That would make us look to look a little less suspicious. Maybe we should all laugh to show we are a team," said The Professor of the *Patali* who was in the Old Man.

"Ha...ha ...ha," the one possessing his wife tried laughing. He started twisting and moving the head weirdly.

"That does look happy. Let us all move our heads like that," another one said.

Soon the group started resembling zombies.

The Buffalo didn't have much of imagination. It neither had much of thought. Its team members were handpicked. They were as clear in thinking like it. All the thinking was usually done by The Professor and The Wind-man.

"Gruuuunnnnnnnnnntttttttt, Excuse me, I wanted to know about this Old Man living in the forests. He used to deliver milk to the townsfolk, before the great shut down, you know," He asked the Old Man.

The Professor of *Patali* was good at this. He had possessed human bodies several times earlier and knew how this worked. He just had to let go a little, for the brain of the occupied to work and it would do the rest.

The body of the Old Man started behaving oddly now. The brain was half in control, the momentum of the possession was still there, with the bizarre mixture, his limbs went crooked, and his mouth contorted. He managed to speak finally, "I am the Old Man."

The Buffalo was good at noticing an improper human behavior. "Ok, the entire group is a little weird. Let us take this group back to the hospital. Analysis can be done there. We need the old man anyway!" instructed The Buffalo to the team.

Chapter 45

The Chariot driver was sitting at an inn outside the kingdom. His chariot was stowed in a stable. He had checked into an inn.

He had a buffalo to keep him company. He had learned not to complain and not to question. Life did throw some surprises at times. What was the point of living if one just spoke to fellow humans every day?

"Wife is always right. That's what my father told. I have been following it till date; heaven knows" he was in a loathing mood.
The buffalo sat there sipping its drink. It was paying him its complete attention. After all, a man talking about his wife requires complete attention.
"Only the other day, I went home, with some chicken and beer. After all, what does a man ask for after a tiring day? What does a man need ultimately? What is it that every man craves for?"
The buffalo looked a little suspiciously at the chariot driver. It seemed to be blushing. The dialog did seem to be heading in some interesting direction.

"Some chicken to eat and some beer to drink" the chariot driver continued.

As they went wooosh, inside the tunnel, below the stone, the Wind-man seemed to be enjoying. It was a spectacle to enjoy too. Looked like a Diwali night with lots of crackers. "What a pleasant climate it is today," his voice echoed.

"You enjoy these things, don't you? What about the impending great war? Isn't this a detour? We seem to be wasting time." The Professor was a bit angry.

He had a lot of control over his emotions. But to his increasing realization, he had realized he was angry which made him furious.

They hit a dead end. There seemed to be nothing but a dark hole. Before they could talk or think about the next step, Whooooooooosh, The Professor and The Wind-man got sucked into it.

"The pressure is tremendous. Let us switch on our safety gears" The Professor went into deep meditation and created a layer of safety around himself.

The Wind-man followed suit. Now they floated through the high-pressure black hole.

And wooosh...

"Where are we?!!" The Professor said with an anxious voice.

For a change, The Wind-man looked a bit anxious too.

Chapter 46

The Chair-man was sitting in his cabin, thinking about things in general. Something felt weird on his head. Like something was crawling. This was happening a lot off late; he heard it from many of his men about this weird crawling feeling. Maybe some new strain of a virus, he had thought. Right now he was thinking, "I have to get hold of The Bangle, I have always wanted The Bangle" He stood up and shouted into the sky. "I will be the Lord of The Bangle."

He took his scribbled notes on the art of war, stood up and rushed outside the cabin. He ran towards the kingdom's gate. A potbellied man running that fast was a scientific miracle. There was hardly anyone interested in looking at the miracle unfold.

As he ran through the gate, he noticed the buffalo and the Chariot Driver sitting outside an inn. He rushed towards them. "You need to let me borrow your buffalo. I have urgent work. It is critical. I will pay you handsomely."

The buffalo did not seem to hear. It took no notice of him and continued sipping its drink. It is suspected that the Buffaloes are the most intelligent species. The way they treat everyone, they have a 'do not-give-a-damn attitude' and they focus on their work; such traits can only be seen in brilliant scientists.

The Chariot driver looked up and was happy to see the additional company "hey, come join us for a drink."

The Chair-man did not have the patience "Listen, I will pay you on my return. I will be the king then. I have to rush and find The Bangle" He started tugging at the buffalo. Next few moments went in a blur. Soon the Chair-man found himself on the ground. His back hurt "I need The Bangle. I will conquer the universe. Attack from the left then the right and then the left" he soon passed out.

"A large number of possessed people are moving towards one place. The rumor about 'The Lord of The Bangle' seems to be working." Inu said in a satisfied tone. Suddenly she noticed it. It took a while for her to process what she just saw. She turned towards Etash in panic. "oh *Eshwara*! Etash!! Look at the monitor for the multiverse!!! It is converging. The entire thing is collapsing! The multiverse is converging."

"Oh man! A story evolves into multiple possibilities and results in the multiverse. Converging of possibilities results in a single universe! This probability never occurred to him.

"Can the single universe sustain the impact of all the converging stories? It looks like a big collapse."

"Oh No! No! No! No! No! Did we end up destroying everything?" Etash panicked.

"Breathe! Breathe!" Inu tried to keep herself in control. "Let's not panic. Listen to me. Not everyone can have the same ambition or same thought. It cannot happen. I guess that's what is referred to as 'rules of nature.' People may decide to go to *Brindavan*, but then some may take a bus, some may take a train. Right now, the multiverse is converging because everybody is heading in one direction and possibilities are reducing. It will expand again when new possibilities come up, possibilities like people meeting with accidents, it raining heavily, or people getting back to their senses." She then thought for a while and continued. Nonetheless, let's help nature a little. We can feed random stories to random minds, thus generating new possibilities."

"No, that would be total chaos. We have done enough damage. Let us not interfere any more now. You have made a great point about the rules of nature. Let the rules take over." Etash looked a bit relieved by Inu's theory. He did not want to interfere with the flow of the great story, and its subplots anymore. "Let the story have its way. Let the things flow the way they want to." He thought with a sigh.

Inu looked at the monitor anxiously. She hoped they had played a constructive role in the evolving story.

Chapter 47

"Our man is here," A hooded figure told another hooded figure as they hurried. It was not clear what they were hurrying towards.

"We can start the process of corruption." They did not notice the oily footsteps leading to a corner. The *Patali* were doing their jobs across the multiverse with enviable dedication.

Yuvan and Isha stared.
Yuvan whispered, "Who are they? This is possibly the tenth group we saw on our way to the palace."
"We can't analyze it and waste our time. We should rush to the palace and tell the king about our great plan. We should inform him about all the stupidity going on."

They started running towards the palace keeping to the dark alleys.
A dark hooded figure followed them.

They had all assembled in a large hall on the ground floor of the hospital. The Buffalo wanted to stall the Old Man and family until The Professor was back. "Would you want to eat something?" It asked the family.

"Eat, with the mouth. To get nutrients. So that the body can survive, yes, yes," said The Professor of *Patali*.

The Buffalo looked at him. Something in the sentence did not seem right. After a brief thought, he just gave up. As you already know, thinking was beyond what he usually did.

He brought some idly from the top floor kitchen.

"White, disk-shaped, hmm.....nice" The *Patali* Professor slowly let the mind of the Old Man take over a little bit. "Oh wow idly after so many days of eating just roots, wow" Spoke the Old Man guided partially by his own mind now. The hand to mouth coordination seemed under control of the Old man's mind as well, though, the face and beard were all messed up at the end of the process.

"What is it you wanted from me?" Asked the *Patali* professor regaining complete control.

"You know this language from Andaman. You have to decipher something written on a stone. My friends will be getting it any moment now." The Buffalo responded. It didn't see any reason to hide any information. The Old Man spoke weird. Then who is he to judge? He had seen enough of weird that weird did not feel weird anymore. So much so, that he actually missed noticing the weird.

"A stone cipher! What does it have?" Old Man's voice controlled by the *Patali* Professor asked.

"Something that explains the secrets of fighting the war with *Patali*. Do you want some coffee? It is brewed from local seeds."

The Professor of *Patali* almost dropped his plate in shock. "War with us?!! We have to destroy this stone!!" he thought.

"Coffee! The hot liquid, with milk and sugar. The bitter drink? Yes!, Yes!" it was the one possessing the wife.

The Professor of *Patali* glared at her "I do the talking here."

He turned to The Buffalo and said, "This secret message on the stone, do you think it still exists? You know, with all the thieves in the town these days."

"What thieves?" The Buffalo smelt something fishy now.

"The town was recently abandoned. I have heard rumors of hidden treasure. Many people have been digging up. They don't seem to find much, but then they are ready to take whatever they can lay their hands on." The Professor was happy. He had developed a story impromptu. He was getting good at the art of possession.

"Do you think the stone would be in danger?" The Buffalo was worried now.

"I do! Moreover, you being so strong and all, just sitting here feeding us, may not be a good idea. You should go and help your friends find the stone. We can accompany you, we can do the decryption right there." The *Patali* Professor seemed excited now. He felt the power. He felt more comfortable in misleading here than in leading in the Patal. This was much easier than that entire leadership thing he had to go back there.

"Alright, but I will lead. I can sense where my friends have gone. You all just follow my tail. No hanky panky then.." The Buffalo got up. It motioned to the Professor's army members to follow as well.

The family followed suit. The Buffaloes were used to making a line, the milkman was used to herding buffaloes, the wife was used to leading her husband, the sons were used to walking here and there, the children, their wives -the zombie tribe went out of the hospital and took a right following the buffalo's tail. The 50,000 strong human Professor's army members followed them.

Chapter 48

They reached the king's bedroom. It was still early. King, being the king, they assumed him to be asleep. So they had directly headed to his bedroom. As they slowly went towards the bed, all the lights of the room switched on. Yuvan stood still, while Isha ran for cover and hid behind a curtain.

"Hmm, I like you, Yuvan. You know when it is too late to hide" It was a woman's voice. It was coming from the doorway. As they waited anxiously, a hooded figure walked in.

"Are you one of the people hurrying around and nothing to do?" Yuvan asked innocently.

"No, I'm one of the people with a lot of things to do" the hooded figure took off the hood and threw off the shawl. She seemed pretty tall. She looked pretty human.

"Who are you?" Yuvan did not recognize her.

"I'm the lead councilor. You need some answers. I owe you some answers."

Isha slowly came out of her hiding "we do not have any presentation."

"Your presentation, as interesting as it may be and as revolutionary as it is considered, we do not need it. Sorry. Things do not work here the way you perceive. We are running this kingdom for several decades without a king. We know how to manage the kingdom on a tight budget. Given an opportunity, people like The Chair-man or The Web-man, would break the kingdom up and sell us in spare parts shop." She paused to assess the reaction of Yuvan and Isha. "We understand your idea would be efficient and can help us if we were to go to war. However, right now we are more interested in keeping an aura of invincibility for the kingdom. Our enemies should be deterred from attacking. Our budgets are sparse, and we are pretty weak. So no war! We just use people like the Chair-man or the Star-boy to keep some rumors going. Neighboring kings will notice that we are preparing something and will be frightened. We will send emissaries and reach an agreement." She was pacing around the room as she spoke. She walked in the king's bedroom as if she owned the place "Having said that, we do see that you and Isha are quite capable and would like to utilize your service. Do join our council as assistants. You will be paid richly."

Isha spoke "We would need some time to think. Can we discuss and get back?"
"Ok, think a lot. Take your own time. However, get back to me by today evening. Rest assured that you couldn't get a better deal. Do not rest though until you have thought from all angles. It should be your decision. If I were you, I would answer immediately."
Yuvan and Isha started to think.

Etash and Inu were relaxing below a tree in the ghost town. They had just returned. After observing the multiverse returning back to normal through the monitor, they had decided to check on The Professor. They were worried that their rumor of stone encryption would have led The Professor and the Wind-man into thick forests.

"Narayana. Narayana" The traveling sage walked towards them.

"Sir" they stood up with respect.

"You guys have done a fabulous job there! I have seen many a Maya, and this impressed me." The sage sat beside Etash as he spoke.

"The Great sage, " Inu referred to him with reverence. "What brings you here?"

"Your jobs are done. Now follow me, let me take you to a very nice spot. You will enjoy watching the war, whenever it happens." The sage said.

"What about The Professor?" Inu sounded worried. "We seem to have led them into thick forests."

"The story has found its way. We are just instruments. The Professor and The Wind-man are far away in some remote universe" The Sage said in an assuring tone as he got up. "Things will be alright. Just follow me." He started chanting. "Narayan...Narayan" With every chant he was rising in the air. At a substantial height, he turned and started walking towards the east and slowly raising further. Etash and Inu followed. They repeated the sage's chant. Soon they had risen to the end of the atmosphere.

"How are we still able to breathe?" thought Etash to himself.

As they walked ahead, Etash and Inu gasped with shock. There, ahead of them, standing magnificently was a huge building. It looked like a Roman theatre. As they went in, they realized it was indeed a theatre, a vast theatre. Something was missing though. There was no stage. It was almost like a planetarium.

"This is the best spot. Narayan Narayan..." the sage showed a row of seats at the center of the theatre. "Do you guys want some popcorn or something to drink maybe?"

Inu and Etash were too mesmerized to speak. They sat watching the stars. Suddenly, two screens materialized in front of Etash and Inu. The screens looked like touch screens of a tablet.

"Narayan...Narayan. Let me help you." The Sage seemed like an expert in these weird, unearthly tablets. He showed them techniques of navigating between different views. They soon realized to their delight that they could watch the entire multiverse by browsing through the screens.

"Hey! I managed to locate The Professor and The Wind-man!!" Inu said with excitement. "But where are they?"

Chapter 49

Earlier, before the presentation from the Star-boy and the Chair-man, the councilors had met. Their secret agent 004 had brought them a secret message.

"So what you say is, the idea and design of the war made by Yuvan are brilliant."

"Yes," 004 was standing very close to the council leader for her comfort. He thought of himself as very charming.
"Hmm, my councilmen. In the long-term, having such an idea would bear fruit. The kingdom could have a strong army and have successful wars. However, I propose we take things slow. This may affect the council. We need to reassert our importance. Let us see if we can get Yuvan on board. Meanwhile, I propose we approve the Chair-man and the Star-boy's proposal, however stupid it may sound. We can approve a small budget keep them on board, scare the neighboring kings and keep peace going. We would be much safer with the Chair-man and Star-boy rather than a confident Yuvan," the councilwoman lead proposed.

The rest of the councilors murmured approval. An open approval was never granted in the history of the council. It should always be like, we knew this already, but we do approve that you were the first to voice it. 'We-are-as-intelligent-as-or-more-than-you' attitude always worked in the council.

"Ohoooo….uhooooo….wakey…wakey"

"What!? Oh, Wind-man. Where…where are we?" The Professor's brain had taken stock now. He had imagined himself as a bear. 'Just a nightmare,' he thought to himself.

"It seems to be a nice place. An island of sorts. The beach is awesome, very clean waters. The board at the beach read 'Seashell-the beach paradise.' There were some sweet drinks in the bar." The Wind-man seemed to blabber.

"What bar? How did we land here?"

"That lady at the bar is charming. I think she likes me."

"Are you even listening to yourself? We have a war at hand. We can't waste time."

"You can't relax, can you?! That is why your hair is all so messy."

The Professor ignored the comment.

"There is a big concert in the evening. Get freshened up quick. We have to go to a beautiful lagoon. The bartender promised to take us there."

"Yeah, whatever. There is no winning with you."

The Professor and the Wind-man soon set off with a young island girl whom The Wind-man introduced as the bartender. They were heading towards the lagoon. The Professor flip-flopped from being in control, to totally being upset with this unknown situation. He kept analysing "We are probably in some land in between. The stone must have closed our direct entry back to earth. This is beyond our strength. If we try to thought travel back, we may end up several years away from the present. We would end up as lost souls in an alien land. The only way to return will be if someone moves the stone. What if the person who moves the stone get sucked in before we can get out?"

"So you use this gel every day? The skin seems very soft. What about your hair? It's like silk, any special shampoo?" The Wind-man was trying to flirt with the bartender.

The young island girl smiled. She never spoke. "So how many of you are here? How big is this place?" The Professor wanted some answers.

She never spoke.

"She doesn't seem to know much. How did you get to know there is a concert?"

"I got this pamphlet at the bar counter. She is cute isn't she?"

"There is something fishy don't you think?"

"Don't be so scared. Let us just have some fun."

The Professor knew the Wind-man very well, too well to bother to react on this.

"The young island girl's smile seems very very odd. Can't say plastic any more after the great plastic ban. Maybe mud like, very organic. Definitely not human, not even a bit. Who would have got us here? It can be a friend who is trying to help, but more so looks to be someone trying to spoil everything. Could it be the *Patali*?" The Professor kept analysing as he walked closely behind the young island girl. "You seem to be a horribly beautiful person with a weirdly pleasant sense of humor" he commented to the young island girl.

"Thank you!, A compliment! Ha..ha", the young island girl finally spoke.

"Hmmm....tick," thought The Professor. He checked his sword in the obfuscated sheath on his back.

The lagoon was beautiful, to say the least. Two huge mountains, clear water, hardly any waves, a penguin doing the backstroke, seemed like a place out of a painting.

"This place looks like 'right-out-of-a-painting. Wait! This is from the greatest painting! Isn't this from a memory from one of our adventures, the adventures of Bali? After the war of Bali, they had wanted to capture the moment. The painter had … - Wait a minute!! Are we in the memory from our past?! This is definitely the handiwork of The *Patali*. "thought The Professor with growing anger.

Meanwhile back on earth, in the present, The Buffalo stood chewing: nothing as usual.

The team behind The Buffalo stood, not sure what to do next.

"Maybe The Buffalo is invoking the secret mantra to make the stone turn," The Professor of *Patali* thought.

The stone had somewhat changed after The Professor and Wind-man had left. Now the flat side was facing the approach pathway, and the other side with scriptures was …...also facing the approach pathway! Some kind of multidimensional display was in front of them now! It had become a kind of multifaceted distortion. Nobody could make out anything on the stone.

The Buffalo continued to chew nothing.

The *Patali* stood behind The Buffalo with patience. The stone had to be destroyed. However, they had to first find The Professor and The Wind-man. They should have been here. "No option but to wait for The Buffalo's next move." thought the Professor of *Patali*.

Chapter 50

"Yuvan! Yuvan! Wakeup! What happened? Aaah!" seeing Yuvan fall down, Isha went to his aid. Now Isha was feeling dizzy too.

This was all too sudden. It started with a feeling that the world was revolving faster than usual. Then it felt like it wasn't anymore. Finally, it looked as if they were being sucked into a funnel.

Isha noticed animals and plants being sucked in as well. They were traveling through a tunnel now. The speed of the travel had reduced. She turned and saw the animals and other humans sucked in, watching them in amazement. Yuvan was fast asleep on her shoulder. She did not feel his weight though.

"Narayana! Narayana!" A sage was traveling with them.
She noticed the councilors there at the back. They were standing in a huddle and discussing the quality of the picture on the LED panel.
"This can be used for playing the videos of the strength of the kingdom. We can have such panels placed near the entrance of the enemy kingdoms." She heard one of the councilors.
"Maybe we can play some movies that would addict their soldiers. We don't have to bother about wars anymore" this was a councilor too.
"We can name it a Darkywood and collect money for every screening. We can make a lot of money." this was the voice of the lead council lady.

Inu was staring at her screen. "This place looks like out of some movie. It can't be from today's universe. Where are they?" She had noticed The Professor and The Wind-man while navigating through various universes randomly.

"Somehow the rumor of the encrypted stone has turned out into a nightmare for The Professor and The Wind-man. Coincidently, there was an encrypted stone in the forest. " The Sage explained. " They have been sucked into a great imaginary past. The *Patali* are preparing for war in their memory. You had a great plan earlier, I must say. But then the story finds its way." The sage continued in a worried tone now "Having a war in the past is a problem. A lot of past memory links could be destroyed. The present universes in the multiverse could get orphaned."

"What?" Etash said in a shocked tone.

"I said there will be a war. However, don't worry. We will handle it." The sage tried to calm him.

"No, I meant, you said, Orphan universe. What is that?"

"Universes with no links to each other. Universes that aren't parallel anymore. The rules of the multiverse do not apply to orphan universes. *Patali* would be free to regain possession of people in the orphan universes," explained the sage.

Etash and Inu further scrolled through the visuals of the multiverse.

Chapter 51

"Hey look at this!" Etash pointed towards the monitor ahead.

"It seems like a stray universe! It's moving randomly. It seems to be...!" Inu almost screamed.

"It is heading straight at us. Maybe one of the parallel universes got untangled when we ran the previous rumor. Will it crash onto us?" He asked the sage in panic.

"Narayana! Narayana! Everything happens for a reason. It is not a parallel universe. It is an orphan universe. A detached universe from long ago. It has grown tangentially from there."

The universe was fast converging now.

"This can be dangerous. We may lose senses when this universe converges into us!! Will we die?"

"It is almost here..." The speech was almost a blur. Everything seemed to blur now. One could see multiple instances of Etash. One could see multiple existences of Inu.

"Aaaahhhhhhhhhh..." Etash seemed to be distorted and screaming in all directions. It looked like he was transforming into an ape and then back as human and then as a cat.

"Aaaahhhhhhhhhh..." Inu seemed distorted in all directions. She transformed into a cat directly. Girls do not see themselves as evolving from apes. That part of the theory is suitable for men.

Then, it was all over. Everything became completely calm.

Inu looked at Etash. He seemed to have changed. He looked the same although.

The Sage smiled "Narayana! Narayana!"

Etash saw Inu. "He was now doubly sure she was his Inu." He saw the beautiful secret agent…he saw the kingdom…he saw the Web-man…he saw himself, and then the confusion was gone. Etash and Yuvan were one now. His mind was clear.

The secret agent opened her eyes. She saw a student, a cute boy whom she had fallen in love with. Were they on the cloud or were they in the kingdom, and then the confusion was gone. Inu, the secret agent had it all clear.

Chapter 52

Wooosh. The stone moved. There was a bright light coming out of the hole below. The *Patali* were all excited. Something was going to happen after all. "Patience pays," is an excellent message. They were now getting a little impatient for the payment. The movement of the stone meant there would be some action.

The Buffalo walked to the hole casually, sniffed, and then turned, slowly bending its hind legs The Buffalo sat in the hole...woosh, and it disappeared.

The Buffalo's team members and then the *Patali* followed suit. Woosh.. Woosh and swish.

They all landed on the beach of Bali. They all landed into a memory of the painting from Bali.

The Professor of *Patali* had a look around, understood the whole scenario, and immediately signalled his team members the coordinates. The war had to begin, right here, in the thought dimension, in the past!

The human Professor saw the newcomers. Face to face with his nemesis, the **Patali** professor. He took his sword out of its sheath. He was ready for the war.

The Wind-man was still lazing beside the girl from the bar counter. "You need to teach me to swim like you someday. The penguin type glide!" He was buried in conversation to notice the newcomers.

Chapter 53

The night was dark. It was as dark as it can get. The web man was dancing. He had web all over him. There was slow music in the background "webify…webify" The voice was gruesome.

The Warrior was held from all sides by the web as well. He could see the king and queen in a corner "pssst…psst"

The Lead of Council Of Ministers, The other Council Of Ministers were looking at the web dance, all-curious.

As the dance progressed, the rhythm got faster "webify…webify…webify"

The Warrior was sweating. "I can't take this anymore" he wanted a way out. He looked around. "A brightly lit tunnel, behind the web man. " Narayana! Narayana!" A voice told behind him. He tugged at the web holding him back. With all his might he pulled. With the last of his will power, he pulled again and lunged forward towards the tunnel. As he was about to enter the tunnel, two pairs of hands held his legs. He risked a glance and noticed The Chairman and The Lead of Soldiers. With all the anger in him, he tugged again and broke free to enter the tunnel. Wooosh…

"Etash…Etash," Inu's voice woke him up. "You have been screaming. What is the matter?!"

"Something is clear…I guess. Just hold me for a while will you?"

Inu hugged Etash tight and held his head to her heart. Etash was soon feeling calm.

"Narayana! Narayana! Such a beautiful sight to see. Oh! Pure love!" Sage's voice. As Inu looked around to see where the sound came from, the door to the men's bathroom opened. The sage walked out.

He came and sat beside Inu. "This is all good. All this romance and all. However, you must know that the war has begun."

"What?!! But..."

"Yes, it has begun. The war is on as we speak. The troika is running havoc on the *Patali*. However, the memories are being cut off as I anticipated. You are needed, Etash. With your newfound knowledge on war, you will be able to save the multiverse. Also, you, my girl! You will run the thought cloud I presume, to provide inputs to our soldiers."

Soon, they were back. Back in the cloud infrastructure. Looking at the monitor on cloud 1.

Etash looked closely at the formations on the monitor. They were showing the enemy lines. The monitor showed the war and status as well. He could see that while the troika was winning, they were exhausting their powers. Additionally, they were only hitting out at the past and a thought world in the past. Regular *Patali* had a very short memory. They preserved their memories in a separate location. Destruction of history would affect humanity. The multiverse was being all messed up already. There were quite a few orphan universes as he could see.

Inu set about pushing thoughts to the orphan universes to connect them back. The sage stood mesmerized by her skills. Woosh, swish, woosh Inu was skilfully rearranging the ideas such that the orphan universes were realigning. However, he could see that this work would soon become difficult and then it would be impossible.

"Hurry up my boy. She can't hold it for long," he urged.

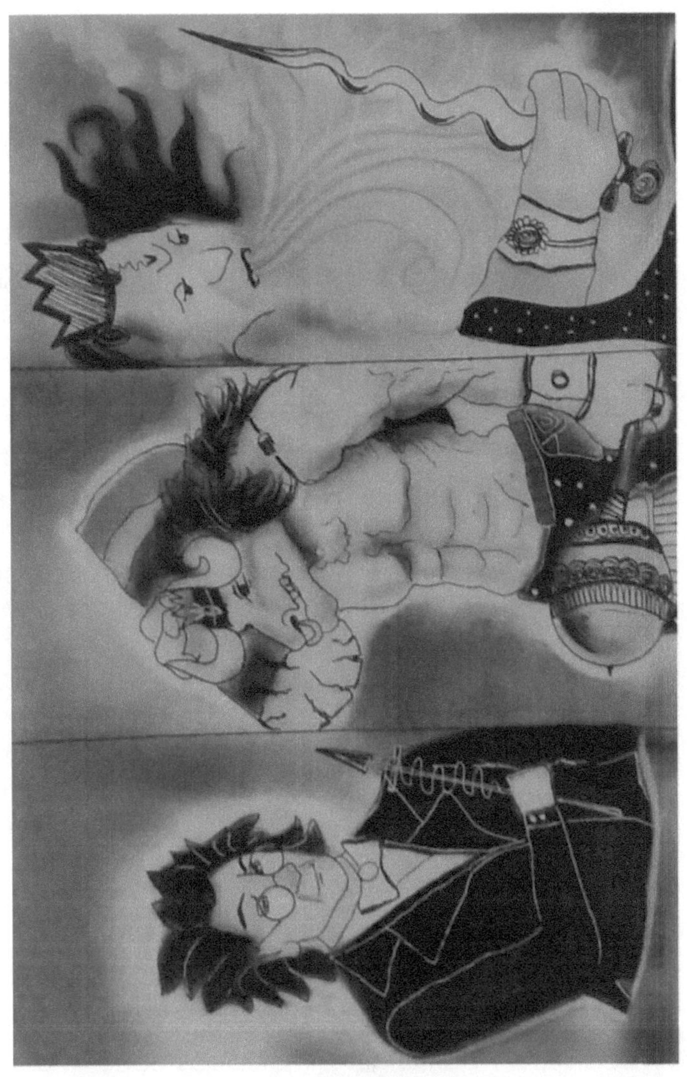

The Troika, Professor, Buffalo and Wind-man

Etash stood on one leg in a prayer stance, folding his hands together and slowly started revolving. The power of Etash mixed with the power of his father and his own intelligence...he was growing large, it seemed like he was growing larger than the universe. The sheer speed of his revolution made him look like a thousand people.

"He is invoking the energy from the 3 energy centers of the universe. From the **Paramaatma** themselves. He is splitting into *Amshas*. He is splitting the energy between different *Amshas*. Art of splitting one's soul!" The sage stood motionless. This was a scene to watch and enjoy.

Meanwhile, the troika and the Patali fought the war bitterly at different levels. They were still in the memory place. They were in the memory from the past. The Buffalo took a big swish holding the sword by its hands. Several *Patali* souls crashed down. It had cut nicely through the *Patali* souls and released them back to Patal.

The Wind-man moved his hands through the air as if slicing it. It released tremendous twisters around him, which killed *Patali* souls near him.

The Professor looked like a Kalaripayuthai expert. He was using the sword presented by the lord. Swish swish. The slice was so precise and thin, *Patali* souls didn't even realize they were free. They stood there for several hours watching the war!

There was destruction all over. It is said that even a small butterfly's flutter can create a tsunami elsewhere. Here the force released by the troika was affecting the place. The memories were being erased, and new ones were being formed.

The troika was too busy to realize the impact.

Etash, splitting into Amshas

The Sage watched a large group of Amshas each split and went to fight the *Patali* in different directions.

"He is opening up new frontiers," thought the sage. "Why would he do that?" He could not understand the whole strategy. He took some popcorn out of one of the shelves and sat on a chair to watch.

Now the *Patali* had to fight on different frontiers. Even outside the thought world in the past. The war was not only on different dimensions it was on in different eras.

There were sweat beads on Inu's forehead. She was clearly struggling. This was slowly getting larger than large. Every moment a new frontier was opening up.

Chapter 54

"During our times summers were very long. Not like this. It was just yesterday that we had the first sun in many months and we already have rains!" An old man under a neem tree was complaining. People were sitting in front of him and listening intently.

One of them said, "Even the days seem to be getting shorter. It was only yesterday when I had my usual Monday bath. Today, my calendar is already alerting me for my next bath."

Many people nodded their head.

"We seem to be losing time. We can't let it happen" The old man sitting at a higher pedestal under the neem tree said.

There was another thunder. This time it was louder.

"Let us approach the history monk." Someone suggested.

Everyone present chorused, "Let us approach the history monk."

They all got up and started walking towards the house of history monk. A more significant thunder, just as they started, made them walk faster. They knew how this would end if the monk did not intervene. They would soon be nothing but pigs grazing on the farm.

The history monk stayed on a small hillock. In fact, it was so small that the monk carried it around when he had work to do. Otherwise, he kept it on the ground and then placed his house on it. The hillock balanced the house pretty well. The monk stayed in the house to be precise.

As they neared his house, they could feel strong vibrations emanating from the house. The door was open. A bright orange light was coming out through the door.

Once there they noticed the monk sitting at the center of the house on the floor. He was rapidly moving the pattern in front of him. Colors seemed to be dancing to his motions. He smiled on seeing them.

"Your times shall soon be restored. Your memories will be fixed. Don't worry. There is this great lady who is working for us. I have never seen such precise work. I'm supporting her with the historical work. You all sleep tight with the knowledge that the lady and I are protecting you."

Chapter 55

"Inu...Can you hear me?" Etash tried to communicate through the thoughts.

"I can't manage this for long. What's happening? "

"We have split up *Patali* into multiple frontiers. They are running thin. It works very well. I should soon be able to overpower them."

Meanwhile, the *Patali* Professor is a worried man. He is with his trusted lead, the lead of his Akshauni army, the trusted lieutenants that he could turn too anytime.

"The only way out of this is to psst...psst" He whispered into the lead's ears.

The leaders knew this approach very well. He had been tuned for this. He quickly arranged for a couple of his trusted men and set out towards the battlefield, the field where the human Professor's men were fighting. As they headed in the direction, they transformed. They transformed into the well-known troika. The *Patali* Akshauni team transformed themselves as the human Professor, the Wind-man and the Buffalo.

"Gentlemen, hold up the war! , the transformed human professor was now addressing the human warriors. "We are being misled. The enemy is within. The very person whom we had trusted, Etash, he is messing up everything. He has joined the *Patali*." The Human Professor spoke to his men. Of course, the actual Human Professor was elsewhere fighting the *Patali*. The human Professor's men stopped.

"The guard is the thief." An *akshauni* shaped as the Buffalo shouted.

The voice reverberated across the human Professor's army. "The guard is the thief."

"In fact, the whole war is a game plan of *Patali* Professor and Etash. This is being done to make Etash the king of all the universes. We are fighting a political war." An *akshauni* shaped as the Wind-man shouted.

The voice sunk deep into the human Professor's army. The shoulders of the human Professor's army sunk as well. Slowly they turned towards each other. Then they turned towards the Akshauni troika shaped as the Professor, Buffalo, and Wind-man. A representative stepped out and spoke "We go back this moment. We don't care for politics. We want justice. If there is no justice to fight for, we do not fight."

"I'm sorry guys. Looks like this is not the right war. Let us all leave" The Buffalo shaped Akshauni encouraged them.

Soon the battlefield was empty. The *Patali* Akshauni soldiers were staring at each other with jubilation. Now the entire energy had to be focused on the real troika. The army was gone.

Chapter 56

The Buffalo, the Professor, and the Wind-man could now feel the effect. Every *Patali* focused on draining them out. The *Patali* were coming near enough to keep them engaged but were far enough to not get hurt. They desperately looked around for their team members. They were all alone. Their army was gone. Somehow, their army had vanished! This is a disaster. Though the troika was fighting the main war, they still needed their army to keep the *Patali* busy. Without their army, they would tire out soon.

At the other end of the war, Etash felt the effect. He felt weak. His *amshas* revolving around him started fading out. The revolution of the *amshas* slowed down and soon stopped. He saw the collapse and looked towards the traveling sage for help. The traveling sage was busy with his bowl of popcorn. He could not understand his sudden loss of power. It looked like the receding army of the human Professor had affected Etash's power.

"Oh, Great Sage! Help! What is happening?" He prayed to the traveling sage. The war looked to be back on track for the *Patali* now.

Chapter 57

The Council Of Ministers from the kingdom found themselves in a lurch. They had always had someone to blame. However, right now there seemed to be no kingdom, no king, and no warriors. It had all suddenly changed. People wore strange clothes. The chariots were weird too! There appeared to be chaos everywhere. They could not understand the magnitude of the change. A crash of two universes was beyond what they could understand.

They headed along the road. Thankfully, people did speak English. The boards were all in English. The lead of the Council Of Ministers read out one of the boards loud "Bangalore Central...hmm, we are somewhere in the center of things. This must be where their kings sit. Let us go and find why things have changed. We need to have a new kingdom soon. We can't survive without a kingdom and a 'notion'-al presence of a king."

They headed in and went to the first shop. It was an electronics shop. They decided to watch and learn.

The salesman was speaking "Sir, latest model washing machine. It rotates at 11,000 rpm. It's motor...blah blah"

The lead of Council Of Ministers walked to the customer. He lifted his hand to hush up the salesman. "Sir, what is your profession may I ask?" He spoke to the customer.

"I'm a businessman. I sell Lassi, buttermilk, etc."

They continued the talk for some time. In the end, the customer bought 50 washing machines. He wanted to expand his Lassi business and what better way to churn the curd than the 11,000 rpm motor!

The Council Of Ministers from the old kingdom had arrived in the new world.

Chapter 58

Etash was desperately calling on the sage. All his efforts seemed to have gone in vain. The *Patali* would win the war, and the multiverse would get into chaos. All this when he could have averted the damage.

Inu noticed the changing fortunes. The number of orphan universes had tripled now, She turned around to notice Etash on his knees. She realized the traveling sage had to be called in. She quickly left the terminal and ran towards the sage.

With updates from Inu, the sage soon realized the situation. Seeing the sudden change in the war scenario, he was shocked. With sage-ly composure, he gathered himself and started meditating to invoke the powers of the pillars of the universe. As the sage meditated, colored circled started emanating from his head. They formed circles around him. Here, nature was probably trying to point out that the sage was indeed holy.

He went back to the time in the hospital when Etash had just arrived. He went back to the time when Etash had arrived back in the hospital with the Wind-man. Every soul cells of the team members of the Professor ticked for Etash. However, the Professor had made Etash a bait by exaggerating his powers up. This had resulted in his people building immense faith in Etash's powers. There is immense power in faith. The power of faith along with the merger of power from Yuvan had transformed Etash into the invincible form of today.

The sage could finally see through the entire game plan of the Akshaunis. The Akshauni's had used their power to weaken Etash and the troika. The rumor had weakened the faith the army had on Etash. Etash had derived his strength from the faith of the army. With that gone, Etash's power had receded. With the army being able to reach the *Patali* positions, it was easy for the troika to attack. Without the army, the troika was left defending themselves from their positions. They would wear out soon. This was all clear now.

"Hmm, one needs all the help to realize one's true potential. However, once you realize the potential, it is up to you to retain it. Power is in you, faith or no faith." The sage thought. "It is high time Etash starts running on his own power." With that thought, he rushed and placed his hand on top of Etash's head. A profound silence enveloped the entire universe. It seemed like the universe was eager to see what happened next.

Slowly Etash started revolving again. The amshas started splitting up as before. Within a few hours, Etash and his amshas had engulfed the entire multiverse as before.

The Professor, The Buffalo, and the Wind-man stood looking at the amshas in action. They could not understand these phenomena playing in front of them. They just stood there speechless. The whole phenomena of such a massive split in amshas were beyond any living being's grasping power. This was at the 64th dimension0. They could see and feel the towering presence of Etash without realizing who or what he was.

Inu ran back to her terminal fearing everything would have gone out of control. She noticed her chair and stood there shocked. An old man was sitting and furiously typing on the keyboard. The old man had a bright light emanating around his head.

He clearly seemed holy. "Who are you?" she managed.

The old man bowed and stood up "oh Inu! The great power of time, the goddess of time. I'm humbled to have met you. I'm the history monk. Sit back and continue. I will work on restoring history." The monk smiled and disappeared.

Chapter 59

The Professor, the Buffalo, and the Wind-man stood in a trance. The surge of the amshas around them had caught them off guard. Their focus had been to somehow keep the war going. All their effort was going into warding off the weapons unleashed on them by the hidden far away *Patali*. Now suddenly everything had stopped. The attack on them had stopped. All there was to be seen was the revolving amshas.

Wrooom! Wrooom!. A slow vibrating noise started. Everyone in the vicinity felt the vibration and the noise. It was as if the noise was deep within. Then the level of noise increased manifold. The Professor understood what was happening. He looked at the Wind-man. The Wind-man had realized it too, he was smiling. They could not hear anything now. Their hairs stood on the head like iron filings attracted to a magnet.

Zooom! With a sudden gush of wind, it all stopped. There was no vibration nor any noise.

The Professor looked at the Buffalo, it stood grazing in a corner.

The Professor looked at the Wind-man. He was relaxing under a tree.

There were no *Patali* around. Only the Professor of *Patali*. He stood a little way away, totally confused. The Professor felt sympathy for the old man. After all, it was supposed to be the man's last war. He walked up to him. " You ok Professor?"

"Oh, Professor! Yes, I'm ok. I guess. What just happened?"

"Nothing much. One of our men used the art of spiritual protection."

"What is that?" The Professor of *Patali* stood confused.

"Well, in simple terms all your *Patali* army are back in Patala. They would be covered in a protective sheath. You do not have an army anymore Professor. You just have citizens of *Patali*. Of course, you may not need those weird bedsheets anymore. The protective sheath would keep your bodies warm. You can wear clothes like us now." The human Professor explained.

"But..what do I say to PSI?" The Professor of *Patali* knew very well where the danger was.

"You can say the human army ran away. You frightened the human army. The Intelligensia would be happy. I'm sure they are intelligent enough to find a victory in a loss." The human Professor offered an olive branch to the *Patali* Professor.

"Yes, Professor. I guess I must say thanks."

"You are welcome, Professor." The human Professor was gracious in victory.

"Professor"

"Professor"

They bowed to each other, one comrade to another.

Chapter 60

Etash observed his work with satisfaction. He had placed the last of **Patali** back in their universe. The sheath of spiritual protection was covering the **Patali** universe entirely. They would not realize the existence of any other universe for at least a few billion years until the sheath wore off.

Inu stood by his side. She had finished connecting the last of the orphan universes. She had found a few stray universes that she let be. The multiverse cannot be perfect, after all. The sage stood behind them. He was smiling.

"Now what?" Inu turned towards Etash and asked.

"I would prefer both of you attend my Monday lecture." The voice came from behind. It was the Professor.

Etash smiled. He realized the completion of the mission. His hands throbbed with the memory of immense energy they had felt moments ago, muscle memory they say.

As he turned, he saw his father standing beside the professor. Soon everybody embraced everybody else. It was reunion time.

Chapter 61

"Narayana! Narayana" The traveling sage is sitting on a high pedestal. Inu and Etash are seated in front of him.

"Oh! Great sage! Please help us" Inu says. "This whole two soul thing is troubling us. We understand Inu is Isha and Yuvan is Etash. However, how did this happen? The misery of not knowing what happened to our previous universes is killing us."

Etash nodded his head and joined his hand in prayer.

The traveling sage smiled. "I understand the trauma that you are undergoing. To understand this phenomenon completely, you would need to attain further self-enlightenment. However, I can provide you some basic information. Universes take birth very frequently. You would know this. Every alternate possibility results in a new universe. The one in which you lived as Yuvan and Isha had cut-off from the main universe. It had grown tangentially giving birth to its own child parallel universes. You can call it an orphan universe. Orphan universes are born when human beings with immense knowledge try to fiddle with the flow of the story. A few hundred years back someone like you tried it and the orphan universe was born." The sage looked at Inu and took a deep breath.

"When we tried our trick with manipulating the story's flow by adding the rumor, we ended up creating a lot of orphan universes. The war in history added to the orphan universe count. I managed to stitch all of them together." Inu knew about the concept of an orphan universe.

"I haven't heard of this concept mentioned anywhere!" Etash sounded surprised.

The sage nodded and continued, "Yes, not many people have known about this concept. There is no record or document of it anywhere. Anyways, Inu managed to salvage the situation and stitch everything up as she mentioned. You must know that universes in parallel tend to merge with each other when possibilities converge. We can call it a safe and natural merger of universes. Now coming back to how you ended up as merged souls. The incident I refer to happened just before the war started. This orphan universe of Yuvan and Isha crashed into our universe when the possibilities for both universes seemed to converge. It was a brutal crash as unlike with parallel universes, Orphan universes have grown very far apart and any convergence can be a catastrophe. I should say we were lucky." The sage again took a break, knowing fully well that the concept may have been difficult to understand.

Inu spoke "When parallel universes converge, we do not even realize. We just have a feeling that we have already been there and done it. Sometimes we call it Déjà vu. When an orphan universe crashes we end up as messed up merged souls."

The traveling sage was impressed with Inu's quick summary "Very aptly put. Don't be very sad about it. You now have an extra brain each. Your friends from the orphan universe, the Web-man and the Chair-man, they ended up in the universe in total confusion. Due to whatever they have merged with, they are now considering themselves as superhuman. The Web-man roams around depositing blobs of web. The Chair-man has got a seat in the parliament. He is now taking that seat and roaming around. Your council of ministers, of course, are doing well. "

With everything crystal clear, Inu and Etash along with Isha and Yuvan bowed to the supreme traveling sage.

Wish To Publish With Us?

We are always keen to look at interesting content across genres. Please email your submission to:

info@tanzpuppen.com

The submission should contain the following:

1. Synopsis — A summary of book in 500 words

2. Sample chapters — Two sample chapters not necessarily in order.

3. About - An interesting note about yourself about 200 words